SCIENTIFIC AMERICAN EXPLORES BIG IDEAS

Smartphone Generation

THE EFFECTS OF SMARTPHONES ON TEENS

The Editors of *Scientific American*

SCIENTIFIC AMERICAN EDUCATIONAL PUBLISHING

New York

Published in 2023 by Scientific American Educational Publishing
in association with **The Rosen Publishing Group**
29 East 21st Street, New York, NY 10010

Contains material from Scientific American®, a division of Springer Nature America, Inc., reprinted by permission, as well as original material from The Rosen Publishing Group®.

First Edition

Scientific American
Lisa Pallatroni: Project Editor

Rosen Publishing
Erica Grove: Compiling Editor
Michael Moy: Senior Graphic Designer

Cataloging-in-Publication Data
Names: Scientific American, Inc.
Title: Smartphone generation: the effects of smartphones on teens / edited by the Editors of Scientific American.
Description: New York : Scientific American Educational Publishing, 2023. | Series: Scientific American explores big ideas | Includes glossary and index.
Identifiers: ISBN 9781684169276 (pbk.) | ISBN 9781684169283 (library bound) | ISBN 9781684169290 (ebook)
Subjects: LCSH: Smartphones–Juvenile literature. | Smartphones and children–Juvenile literature. | Smartphones–Psychological aspects–Juvenile literature. | Smartphones–Social aspects–Juvenile literature.
Classification: LCC TK6564.4.C45 S637 2023 | DDC 004.167–dc23

Manufactured in the United States of America
Websites listed were live at the time of publication.

Cover: Ground Picture/Shutterstock.com

CPSIA Compliance Information: Batch #SACS23.
For further information, contact Rosen Publishing at 1-800-237-9932.

CONTENTS

INTRODUCTION

Since smartphones were introduced to the public in the early twenty-first century, these devices have represented an abrupt shift in the way we communicate and socialize with others, seek out and absorb information, and find entertainment. Suddenly, all of this became available with the click of a button. However, while these devices had a transformative effect on the lives of those who grew up in the pre-smartphone era, for today's generation of teenagers, smartphones have been a ubiquitous presence throughout their lives. Consequently, scientists, health care professionals, and the general public have developed an interest in–and concern about–the effects a lifetime of smartphone use has had on today's teenagers from a mental health, social, and neurodevelopmental perspective.

The articles in this book attempt to reflect the varied and evolving attitudes toward teen smartphone use while presenting scientific research aimed to consider the ways in which smartphones affect a teen's brain and mental health. Section 1, "Your Brain on Smartphones," features articles that examine the question of how smartphones affect the brain and reflect the shifting attitudes on the impacts of smartphone use. Section 2, "Virtually Socialized," looks at the ways in which smartphones have changed how we socialize with one another, particularly through the use of social media. Section 3, "How Smartphones Affect Mental and Physical Health," looks at research and opinions on the impacts that smartphone use has on mental and physical health, particularly for teens. Finally, Section 4, "Smartphones and the Sharing of Information and Opinions," considers how smartphones and social media have changed the way we communicate our knowledge and perspectives with one another in the smartphone era. Through examining the question of how smartphones have changed the way people think, feel, and communicate from a variety of viewpoints, this book aims to illuminate how these devices have impacted the smartphone generation.

Section 1: Your Brain on Smartphones

Are Smartphones Really Destroying the Lives of Teenagers?

By Carlin Flora

Is any age group more maligned than teenagers? As they roam in packs, they're feared, avoided or told to calm down. They're gawky, narcissistic, hormone-addled, shallow, angsty and entitled. And on top of all that: Have you heard? Smartphones are destroying their brains. Raised in the glow of digital devices, today's teens are depressed, anxious, antisocial and hopelessly distracted.

Smartphones have become a touchstone of adolescence in large part because they are nearly ubiquitous. As of 2015, 73 percent of teenagers in the U.S. had a smartphone, and, as of 2016, 84 percent of American households contained one, according to a new report from the Pew Research Center. With so many devices at their disposal, a full 92 percent of teens–defined in this report as those ages 13 to 17–report going online daily, including 24 percent who say they do so "almost constantly." Only 12 percent say they go online just once a day.

The latest headlines about teenagers imply that their beloved smartphones are making them mentally ill and socially isolated. Notably, a study published online in 2017 in *Child Development*, led by Jean Twenge, a professor of psychology at San Diego State University, found that today's teens are less likely to drink, have sex, get pregnant, drive, date and work than previous generations. Writing for a general audience in the *Atlantic*, Twenge spun these ostensibly positive trends as something ultimately negative: a worrying reluctance to grow up. She wove in some stats indicating poorer mental health among teens and pinned the gloomy picture on smartphones. "There is compelling evidence," she wrote, "that the devices we've placed in young people's hands are having profound effects on their lives–and making them seriously unhappy."

A month later a *New York Times Magazine* cover story reported on an alarming rise of students with "overwhelming anxiety" on college campuses and named social media as a contributing factor. These stories are just the recent wave. Clinical psychologist Sherry Turkle of the Massachusetts Institute of Technology generated dozens of headlines when she published her 2015 book *Reclaiming Conversation: The Power of Talk in a Digital Age*. She argued that teenagers and adults alike are losing their abilities to understand and pay attention to one another because of the disjointed and solitary nature of electronic communications. These are the abilities, Turkle says, that make us human.

But perhaps unsurprisingly, the generations of adolescents who have come of age in the smartphone era–younger millennials and their successors, Generation Z–aren't irreparably or even especially ruined. And smartphones aren't the clean, easy culprit for behavioral changes observed in 21st-century teenagers. "Over the same time period that Twenge refers to, there have also been improvements in mental health," says Laurence Steinberg, a professor of psychology at Temple University, who studies adolescent development. Two years ago Twenge herself published a study with two colleagues that concluded that today's teens are happier and more satisfied with life than their predecessors.

Parsing these trends is tough because researchers focus on different aspects of mental health using various measurements. But casting "kids today" in a negative light is a time-honored activity. "Every time there's a new form of entertainment or technology, some adult says, 'This is killing our kids,'" says Steinberg, who is also author of *Age of Opportunity*, a 2014 book focused on adolescents' great capacity for change. "They said it about dime-store novels and rock and roll and computers. Young people around the world have survived all these things, and I'm sure they'll survive smartphones."

The very quality that makes teens adaptable is, however, what makes them vulnerable. At the onset of puberty, adolescent brains show heightened plasticity–an increased likelihood to rewire. Driven to seek out novelty and risks, teenagers have flexible neural circuits that help them adjust to environments as they make decisions and learn. As they enter adulthood, the window where connections between brain structures are forged starts to close, hardening their behaviors. "Any experience that people have during the time when the brain is malleable has the potential to affect it," Steinberg says. Kids' brains are affected by all kinds of factors, including parents, friends and school. "Smartphones are not going to have some special significance. That said, the things people spend more time doing have a greater effect on their brains."

Scientists are only just beginning to figure out how smartphone use might affect adolescent development, both behaviorally and neurologically. What is clear is that the extent to which these digital devices are affecting teenage minds is dependent on how kids use smartphones, what they are not doing because of smartphone use, and the social context in which they use smartphones both at home and beyond.

What We Know and What We Don't

In 2015 Lauren Sherman, now a postdoctoral fellow at Temple, witnessed firsthand the misplaced panic around smartphones and teens. Knowing that teens are reward-happy–they show greater activation in the reward regions of their brains than either children or adults–she wanted to explore neural responses to social media "likes." Sherman invited a group of high school students into the laboratory to look at a version of Instagram while inside an MRI scanner. She had manipulated a set of her own posts so that some subjects would see them with a high number of "likes," whereas others would see them with just a few "likes." Subjects submitted their own pictures for the study as well.

The subjects were more likely to "like" pictures if they believed the images were already popular. They also showed more activation in regions involved in social cognition and visual attention, as though they were thinking more about the highly liked pictures and scrutinizing them. When the subjects' own photos received a lot of "likes," they showed a response in the ventral striatum, a brain region involved in reward. "That might explain why teens are particularly avid users of social media and why they find it so motivating," Sherman says.

When the study was released in *Psychological Science*, hyperbole set in. "Because it involves the same brain circuitry, the press was saying that 'likes' are just like crack cocaine," Sherman says. "They aren't! Not even a little bit." A New Jersey television station went so far as to declare that "likes" are better than drugs and sex.

Sherman herself enthusiastically pored over printed-out transcripts of AOL Instant Messenger chats as a teenager. She thinks the "do-do-loo" jingle that signaled a new chat message back then is not so different from a modern teen's "likes." "Neither of these cues is inherently rewarding, like sugar is, but we learn that they represent a social reward," she says. Whether it's a pebble thrown against a window at night or a long-awaited ring of the rotary phone, we can safely assume that any sign of an impending social interaction has long excited teen brains.

Unlike a rotary phone or a desktop equipped with AIM, though, smartphones are practically appendages, a fact that fuels anxiety about what they're doing to teenagers. "We don't have much clear evidence about how smartphone use is affecting brain development," says Nicholas Allen, director of the Center for Digital Mental Health at the University of Oregon. "Anyone who tells you otherwise is speculating," Steinberg agrees: "There is a growing literature, but it's still quite correlational." Even those correlational results are a mixed bag of positive and negative findings, with some studies pointing to the risks of cyberbullying and others highlighting helpful online resources for teens struggling with personal issues.

Long-term research that could show causality would be hard to execute. "You can't randomly assign kids to have a phone or not," Steinberg says. Studying teenagers requires obtaining their parents' permission—an extra logistical challenge. That means that expert predictions are often extrapolations of research on college students. "Sometimes we have good reason to think that the findings from research on young adults may generalize to younger teens, but we have no way of knowing for sure." Complicating matters is the finding that some brain structures, such as the prefrontal cortex, don't fully develop until the mid-20s.

Another research design challenge hinges on what exactly a "smartphone" is. It's a telephone, a camera, a game console and an encyclopedia. Even zeroing in on specific apps teens favor, such as Snapchat and YouTube, is insufficiently broad. "When you're asking how kids are being affected by social media," Steinberg says, "it's like asking about the effect of TV without distinguishing between *Jersey Shore* and *Masterpiece Theatre*."

Of the emerging narratives surrounding Gen Z youth, one of the most pervasive is that they are more depressed and anxious and that smartphone use is to blame. The reality is that "there is a small yet persistent cross-sectional relation between the amount of time spent online and depression and anxiety," Allen says, "but we can't assume it's causal." ("Time spent online" is defined differently, too, with some studies focusing on games or social media alone.) One plausible hypothesis, Steinberg says, is that the causal relation runs in the opposite direction. "It isn't hard to imagine a depressed teenager would rather spend time in her bedroom, online, than go to a social gathering with people from school."

Larry D. Rosen, a professor emeritus of psychology at California State University, Dominguez Hills, and co-author of the 2016 *The Distracted Mind: Ancient Brains in a High-Tech World*, suspects that while it is possible that kids who are already depressed or anxious use smartphones differently, the influence probably goes both ways. Rosen thinks that social comparison (where social media browsers feel awful about their lives after getting bombarded with rosy versions of everyone else's) and emotional contagion (where negative online outbursts affect browsers' states of mind) are possible culprits. Whether or not a teen experiences a self-esteem dip or secondhand moodiness comes down to who they're associating with online and what exactly they're looking at.

It is that precise aspect of how social media is used that researchers are now testing. Oscar Ybarra of the University of Michigan and his colleagues found that subjective well-being was negatively affected by passive use of social media sites because comparisons sparked envy. But active use–posting content and interacting with others rather than just "lurking"–predicted higher levels of subjective well-being, seemingly because active use creates social capital and makes users feel more connected to other people. In another example, a study by the Harvard Graduate School of Education found that teens who were successfully prompted to critically analyze Instagram streams–acknowledging that the images are "curated" and not representative of reality–had fewer bad feelings, particularly if they previously compared themselves negatively with those in their feed.

Although teens' moods may be generally resilient to the vicissitudes of social media, other areas of cognitive development are a growing concern. Temple psychologists Harry Wilmer and Jason Chein found a correlation between heavier smartphone use and less of an ability to delay gratification, for example, taking a smaller sum of money in the moment rather than waiting for a larger amount. Researchers do not yet know if impulsive people are more into phones, though, or if phones are making everyone less capable of resisting urges.

For Rosen, a big concern is not just how teens are using their phones but rather the "technological anxiety" and nomophobia (the feeling someone gets in the absence of their phone), that distract them from other tasks. Research has shown that multitasking leads to worse performance on any of the tasks in play. Using an app, Rosen monitored how many times his students unlocked their phone each day. "It was 50 times, on average," he says, "and they stayed on the phone for about five and a quarter minutes each time." Most of the near-constant checking in had to do with communication because their top apps were Facebook, Instagram, Snapchat and YouTube. "We know that half of the time people check in, it's because they get an alert or notification." Adults seem to be affected, too: a British study showed that just the presence of a phone on a table between two people chatting about a meaningful topic had a negative effect on closeness and conversation quality. The call of the phone is cognitively loud, even when it's turned off.

Temporary distraction is one thing; potential long-term brain damage from stress is more unsettling. "What I'm convinced is happening," Rosen says, "is that after someone checks in [then stops looking at the phone], cortisol leaks into the system out of the adrenal glands. A little bit of cortisol is fine, but a lot of cortisol is not. As the cortisol builds up, people get anxious. The only way to quell that feeling is to check the phone again."

Rosen wonders if the steady stream of cortisol will affect the development of the prefrontal cortex–the part of the brain responsible for, among other things, impulse control and decision making. It is the last part of the body to get fatty cells wrapped around its neurons, a process called myelination. "My guess is that young people are using their prefrontal cortex differently and perhaps less efficiently." He is looking at the prefrontal cortices of "heavy" and "light" tech users with functional near-infrared spectroscopy and has found that, at least while performing one executive functioning task, light versus heavy smartphone users use their prefrontal cortices differently.

Digital Lives, IRL Trade-Offs

Smartphone-wielding teens have been portrayed as reclusive, lacking in empathy, and even incapable of having "real" relationships with friends or romantic partners. The fear is that smartphone use discourages–or replaces–healthy behaviors, including face-to-face interactions (IRL–"in real life"–as the kids say).

Researchers who study teenagers are not so worried. "There's no evidence that using social media impairs the development of social skills," Steinberg says. "The main people kids interact with over social media are the same people they interact with face-to-face." The irony, according to Allen, is that the opportunity to explore relationships of all kinds, without being under the direct watch of their parents, is what draws many teenagers to their phones in the first place. Connecting via smartphones may even improve empathy.

In 2016 a Dutch study surveyed 942 adolescents and then again a year later. Social media use appeared to improve their ability to understand–and to share the feelings of–their peers during that time frame. Whereas another of Sherman's studies on how social media affects intimacy did show that in-person chats between two female teenagers yielded the highest level of connectedness, it wasn't much higher than when they chatted over video. As communication platforms become increasingly audiovisual, Sherman thinks those shifts could bring us all closer together.

But what about incessant texting? Jay Giedd, director of child and adolescent psychiatry at the University of California, San Diego, says teenagers tend to get better at reading facial expressions in their 20s anyway. As for how they are interacting, "you shouldn't confuse 'different,' with 'defective,'" he says. "Some say their texting style is wrong, but they're communicating ideas, even if their prose and grammar are not what we'd like them to be." Instead of looking for deficits, Giedd asks about the trade-offs: "What are their brains better at instead? Sorting through texts? Keeping track of more friends?"

Even the assumption that face-to-face interactions are more satisfying and profound is not always true. Sherman asked her subjects whether there are certain topics they feel more comfortable talking about via digital communications such as texting. They said that if they wanted to say something really emotional and felt like they might cry, they preferred texting. Particularly because they are often interacting online with real-life friends, a different and maybe even deeper mode of bonding can take place as teens trade disclosures that are difficult to say out loud.

Less benign than texting is the unprecedented access to porn smartphones provide, which might affect how many teens, especially those with other risk factors, develop romantic relationships in real life. "Though there's no clear evidence, unrestricted exposure to porn could influence their understanding of sexuality and relationships, especially if it's their earliest exposure to sex," Allen says. A 2016 study found that about three quarters of teenagers (gender or background made no difference) reported a sexual problem such as low desire or inability to achieve orgasm, with clinically significant levels of distress associated with it. The study's author, Lucia O'Sullivan, a professor of psychology at the University of New Brunswick in Canada, says that most young people actually tend to habituate to porn. She thinks that general mental health issues and a focus on pregnancy and infection in sex education–rather than a broader exploration of communication and the "how to" of sexual interactions–are more to blame for her finding.

As teens navigate the complex world of sexuality and relationships of all kinds, they are also "finding themselves." Forming an identity is a big job for teens, and some wonder if smartphone immersion might hinder opportunities for them to come into their own. "Social media is a place where teens are expressing themselves and thinking about how they're presenting themselves to others," Sherman says. "One of the early hypotheses was that teens would go online and explore brand new identities, to become somebody else. That largely doesn't seem to be the case." That doesn't mean they aren't testing slightly different versions of a core identity, though.

Teens are skilled at evading detection and savvy to the cultivation of both public and private selves. "Teens sometimes have their public profile and then a 'Finsta,' or fake Instagram account, where they paradoxically show their real selves," sharing silly faces or unedited streams of thoughts, Sherman says. The trend has likely influenced the functionality of Instagram. "Now it's possible to link two accounts, which was probably a direct response to users creating secondary accounts," she adds. "Adolescents bend these online environments to fit their own purposes. We spend a lot of time talking about the effects of social media on teens, but teens are interacting with these tools–and changing them. It's a bidirectional relationship."

Theo Klimstra, an associate professor of developmental psychology at Tilburg University in the Netherlands, sees smartphones as a double-edged sword for identity formation. "One thing that teens typically do is look for people who are like them, to find a mirror," he says. If you grow up in an area where there are very few people like you, then social media makes it possible to find a kindred spirit. Many researchers point to the example of gay teens who do not feel they can come out in their own towns but can find positive role models and communities online. The potential downsides, Klimstra says, are the tyranny of choice and the possibility of soul-crushing feedback. The Internet could paralyze teens with its overwhelming array of possible selves and damage their self-esteem with extreme reactions on social media.

Even if smartphones are not making teens antisocial or (more) confused about who they are, they do seem to be stealing one adolescent essential: sleep. Overall, teens are sleeping less than in the past. A summary of data on 690,747 children from 20 countries, dating from 1905 to 2008, found that they sleep more than an hour less than young people did 100 years ago.

Sakari Lemola, an assistant professor of psychology at the University of Warwick in England, recently found that teenagers with smartphones fall asleep later at night. "This is probably because they're engaging with social media, communicating with friends and watching YouTube," Lemola says. "We also found that electronic media use around bedtime was related to decreased sleep duration and increased symptoms of insomnia. Short sleep and poor sleep quality were in turn related to depressive symptoms."

There are several possible connections, Lemola says. Modern flat screens emit a larger amount of blue light, which suppresses melatonin, a hormone produced by the pineal gland at night or in the dark that regulates our internal clocks. Getting messages or comments from friends on social media is arousing for teens and makes it more difficult for them to fall asleep. And it's hard to shut off the phone when endless entertainment beckons.

Lemola points to another recent study showing that, in young adults, poor sleep is a contributing causal factor for serious mental health problems such as psychotic symptoms. "On the one hand, I'm confident there is a majority of teenagers who are able to adjust well to the new opportunities offered by social media," he notes. "On the other hand, there is a minority of more vulnerable teenagers who are at higher risk for poor mental health compared with generations before them. It is likely that increases in electronic media use and decreases in sleep quality and sleep duration have played a core role in mental health, although other changes in the lives of teenagers, from urbanization to stress at school, can also play a role."

When Steinberg is flagged down by a concerned, stressed-out parent, he asks, "'What is your child not doing because she's spending time on her phone?' If she's not sleeping, exercising, studying, and stimulating her mind with novel and challenging activities, then that's not healthy." Beliefs about what constitutes "novel and challenging" might also be shifting, though. "Before if someone asked me what's better for a teen: a violin or the video game Assassin's Creed, I'd think it was a joke question," Giedd says. "But I've come to see that Assassin's Creed requires strategy, memory, pattern recognition and reflex skills. And watching well-produced videos is probably a better way to learn than reading. Those words are hard for me to say, but in terms of how the brain absorbs information, it might be true."

Adults These Days

When it comes to the threats that teenagers face, shiny new technologies are a more interesting focal point than familiar and entrenched ones. That bias can skew our sense of proportion: along with poor sleep, Allen says, family conflict is a key source of mental health problems for teens. "Conflict and stress affect the brain, as does a lack of warmth and support. Why worry about the effect of phones when we have so much evidence for these other factors?" Steinberg agrees, saying the issues we should be focused on are trauma, poverty, exposure to violence and hard drug use because they have a huge influence on teenage development.

Smartphone anxiety could simply be a cover for the difficult parts of watching a child change and grow up. "We see that our kids are not as interested in spending time with us or are engaging in some kind of deviant behavior–all those things we associate with adolescence generally," Sherman says. But instead of accepting the changes as normal, "we say, 'Okay, what's different? Oh! It's this new technology.'" After all, Gen X-ers and Millennials spent their teen years glued to the television or immersed in primitive iterations of electronic communications.

It is also helpful to take the anthropological view, Klimstra says. Today's teenagers are "growing up in a very different world. From our perspective, selfies and social media might look narcissistic, but it's all context-related." And theirs is a context infused with economic insecurity. "Unemployment is high in many parts of the world. It makes it really hard to start a life as young person, to get away from your parents, and to become financially and psychologically independent," Klimstra adds. "That's more of a threat than smartphone use."

Researchers do see opportunities to temper the negative effects of smartphone use. Rosen urges teens to "not be a Pavlov's dog and turn off the notifications." He also advises parents to model good behavior by not yanking out their own phones so much. It is a big unanswered question: How are smartphone-obsessed parents affecting teenage brain development if they themselves are less engaged and present with their kids?

"In the U.S., parents give young people a phone at 12 and say, 'Good luck with fake news, bullying and porn.'" Allen says. "We expect teens to grow up immediately and deal with the adult world. We should scaffold those experiences and shape them successively over time, allowing teenagers to be more and more independent. It's clearly an area where education and public policy come into play." Giedd agrees: "The most sought-after therapist in the world isn't Dr. Phil, it's Siri. She fields more mental health questions than anyone. That's not Apple's responsibility. How can we do better if this is where teens are going to turn?"

Because researchers agree that having a close and caring relationship with parents is one of the most important contributors to an adolescent's positive mental health, the best thing parents can do is bond with their teens around tech use. "Ask what they find compelling about their phones," Allen says. "Ask them what their fears and their interests are. That kind of discussion is much more productive than saying, 'Put the phone down at the table.'"

A little faith in scrappy teen spirit can also offset smartphone panic. "The reason we're here and Neandertals aren't is because we have teenagers," Giedd says. "Neandertals didn't really have teenagers; at 12 they had their own children. Neandertal tool use didn't change at all for about 200,000 years. Their brains were bigger than ours, but what they couldn't do is adapt when the climate started changing. By its very design, the teen brain adapts to its environment. Today's teenagers might not memorize how high mountains are and how long rivers are, but they will be able to find the signal in the noise."

The Key to a $300-Million Study of Teen Brains? Smartphones

What if the oft-maligned smartphone could protect teenagers' mental health and help researchers learn about other aspects of adolescent development?

At least 50 percent of mental illnesses start by age 14, and 75 percent start by age 24, a fact that Jay Giedd, director of child and adolescent psychiatry at the University of California, San Diego, has spent his career trying to unpack. The reason symptoms emerge at that time has to do with the plasticity of teen brains and the dynamic changes occurring during this period, which is also why they respond well to treatment. That is, when they get help: "The average time between when someone gets depression and when they get treatment is 10 years," Giedd says. "It's the shame of our profession. One in seven kids is depressed," and very few are getting treatment.

The symptoms of mental illness are often things such as moodiness, which all teens experience. "How do you know if a teen is just being a teen? I've been a psychiatrist for almost 30 years, and it's hard to tell," Giedd says. "The key to diagnosis is change. But the baseline might be all over the place–some people are outgoing; others are shy. If we have someone come in only once every six months, and we ask them, 'How happy have you been?' you're lucky if you get how happy they were that morning."

Enter smartphones: by tracking a teen's online activity, researchers can detect changes because there is a reliable baseline. As such, Giedd is optimistic that mobile technologies could one day help teens more than medications.

Now a landmark project is testing such applications to see the effects of smartphones–alongside other factors–on teen brains over time. The ABCD (Adolescent Brain Cognitive Development) study has received funding of $300 million, "which is more than the entire history of adolescent research around the world up to this point," Giedd says.

The study is headquartered in San Diego but will unfold at 21 sites around the country. The team has so far recruited about 7,000 nine- and 10-year-olds (the target is 11,500) who will be followed for at least the next 10 years. Their brains will be scanned every two years, and they will be tracked by smartphones and other apps every three to six months. The first round of data was released in December 2017, and all data will be freely available for other researchers to use.

Giedd predicts that the brain scans will show subtle but real changes over time, not in the size of brains but in the ways they are connected. "The amount of data coming into our world has vastly increased, and I think that will show up in parts of the brain that deal with prioritizing and scanning. It's possible it will be to the point where you can say, 'Here's a digital-age brain, and here's a non-digital-age brain.' But even with autism and schizophrenia, we can't really do that."

About the Author

Carlin Flora is a freelance writer and author of Friendfluence: The Surprising Ways Friends Make Us Who We Are *(Doubleday, 2013).*

Social Media Has Not Destroyed a Generation

By Lydia Denworth

Anxiety about the effects of social media on young people has risen to such an extreme that giving children smartphones is sometimes equated to handing them a gram of cocaine. The reality is much less alarming.

A close look at social media use shows that most young texters and Instagrammers are fine. Heavy use can lead to problems, but many early studies and news headlines have overstated dangers and omitted context.

Researchers are now examining these diverging viewpoints, looking for nuance and developing better methods for measuring whether social media and related technologies have any meaningful impact on mental health.

It was the headlines that most upset Amy Orben. In 2017, when she was a graduate student in experimental psychology at the University of Oxford researching how social media influences communication, alarming articles began to appear. Giving a child a smartphone was like giving a kid cocaine, claimed one. Smartphones might have destroyed a generation, said another. Orben didn't think such extreme statements were warranted. At one point, she stayed up all night reanalyzing data from a paper linking increases in depression and suicide to screen time. "I figured out that tweaks to the data analysis caused major changes to the study results," Orben says. "The effects were actually tiny."

She published several blog posts, some with her Oxford colleague Andrew K. Przybylski, saying so. "Great claims require great evidence," she wrote in one. "Yet this kind of evidence does not exist." Then Orben decided to make her point scientifically and changed the focus of her work. With Przybylski, she set out to rigorously analyze the large-scale data sets that are widely used in studies of social media.

The two researchers were not the only ones who were concerned. A few years ago Jeff Hancock, a psychologist who runs the Social Media Lab at Stanford University, set an alert to let him know when his research was cited by other scientists in their papers. As the notifications piled up in his in-box, he was perplexed. A report on the ways that Facebook made people more anxious would be followed by one about how social media enhances social capital. "What is going on with all these conflicting ideas?" Hancock wondered. How could they all be citing his work? He decided to seek clarity and embarked on the largest meta-analysis to date of the effects of social media on psychological well-being. Ultimately he included 226 papers and data on more than 275,000 people.

The results of Orben's, Przybylski's and Hancock's efforts are now in. Studies from these researchers and others, published or presented in 2019, have brought some context to the question of what exactly digital technology is doing to our mental health. Their evidence makes several things clear. The results to date have been mixed because the effects measured are themselves mixed. "Using social media is essentially a trade-off," Hancock says. "You get very small but significant advantages for your well-being that come with very small but statistically significant costs." The emphasis is on "small"–at least in terms of effect size, which gauges the strength of the relation between two variables. Hancock's meta-analysis revealed an overall effect size of 0.01 on a scale in which 0.2 is small. Przybylski and Orben measured the percent of variance in well-being that was explained by social media use and found that technology was no more associated with decreased well-being for teenagers than eating potatoes. Wearing glasses was worse. "The monster-of-the-week thing is dead in the water," Przybylski says.

Furthermore, this new research reveals serious limitations and shortcomings in the science of social media to date. Eighty percent of studies have been cross-sectional (looking at individuals at a given point in time) and correlational (linking two measures such as frequency of Facebook use and level of anxiety but not showing that one causes the other). Most have relied on self-reported use, a notoriously unreliable measure. Nearly all assess only frequency and duration of use rather than content or context. "We're asking the wrong questions," Hancock says. And results are regularly overstated–sometimes by the scientists, often by the media. "Social media research is the perfect storm showing us where all the problems are with our scientific methodology," Orben says. "This challenges us as scientists to think about how we measure things and what sort of effect size we think is important."

To be clear, it is not that social media is never a problem. Heavy use is associated with potentially harmful effects on well-being. But effects from social media appear to depend on the user–age and mental health status are two important factors that make a difference. Also, cause and effect appear to go in both directions. "It's a two-way street," Hancock says.

The hope is that the field will use these new findings to embark on a new science of social media that will set higher standards for statistical analysis, avoid preposterous claims, and include more experimental and longitudinal studies, which track people at multiple time points. "We don't want to be a field in which we say that potato eating has destroyed a generation," says clinical neuropsychologist Tracy Dennis-Tiwary of Hunter College. "Despite our concerns, we need to pull ourselves together and act like scientists. We have to have adequate evidence."

Fear of Technology

Anxiety and panic over the effects of new technology date back to Socrates, who bemoaned the then new tradition of writing things down for fear it would diminish the power of memory. Thomas Hobbes and Thomas Jefferson both warned that communal relationships would suffer as industrial societies moved from rural to urban living. "Before we hated smartphones, we hated cities," write sociologists Keith Hampton of Michigan State University and Barry Wellman of the NetLab Network, based in Toronto, both of whom study the effects of technological innovation. Radio, video games and even comic books have all caused consternation. Television was going to bring about the dumbing down of America.

Even so, the change that came about from mobile phones, the Internet and social networking sites feels seismic. Cell phones were first widely adopted in the 1990s. By 2018, 95 percent of American adults were using them. Smartphones, which added instant access to the Internet, entered the mainstream with the introduction of the iPhone in 2007, and now more than three quarters of U.S. adults have them. Eighty-nine percent of those adults use the Internet. There is near saturation for all things digital among adolescents and adults younger than 50 and among higher-income households. Nonusers tend to be older than 65, poor, or residents of rural areas or other places with limited service. Between 2005, when the Pew Research Center began tracking social media use, and 2019, the proportion of Americans using social media to connect, keep up with the news, share information and be entertained went from 5 to 72 percent–that means it jumped from one in 20 adults to seven in 10.

Because social media is so new, the science investigating its effects is also new. The earliest study Hancock could find that examined social media use and psychological well-being was done in 2006. It came as no surprise that early approaches were limited. Physician Brian Primack, who headed the Center for Research on Media, Technology, and Health at the University of Pittsburgh until moving to the University of Arkansas this year, likens the field to initial research on nutrition: "It took a while to say, 'Let's split out fats and proteins and carbohydrates, and not just that, but let's split out trans-fats and polyunsaturated fats,'" he says. "It's important for anyone who is doing good research to adapt to what's going on." Primack points to his own early work, such as studies that looked only at overall social media use, as examples of what will not cut it anymore. "You might be spending two hours a day clicking 'like' on pictures of cute puppies, and I might be spending two hours a day having violent clashes about politics and religion and other hot-button issues. Studies like my early one would count [those activities] the same."

Many people in the field have been particularly critical of work by psychologist Jean M. Twenge of San Diego State University. In addition to her research papers, Twenge's popular 2017 article in the *Atlantic*, based on her book *iGen*, was the one that asked: "Has the Smartphone Destroyed a Generation?" Twenge is hardly the only researcher to publish negative findings about social media use, but the publicity around her work has made her one of the most high profile. She points to a steep rise in mental health issues among the group born between 1995 and 2012 and writes that "much of this deterioration can be traced to their phones." Her work compares rising rates of depression and anxiety among young people to the proliferation of smartphones in the same time period. Twenge acknowledges that the link is correlational but argues that her conclusions represent "a logical sequence of events" based on the evidence–and care is warranted: "When we're talking about the health of children and teens, it seems to me we should err on the side of caution."

No one disagrees about the importance of young people's health, but they do think that Twenge has gotten ahead of the science. "Why wait for causal evidence?" says Dennis-Tiwary. Because the story might not be so straightforward. She points to a longitudinal study done by researchers in Canada in response to one of Twenge's articles. They studied nearly 600 adolescents and more than 1,000 young adults over two and six years, respectively, and found that social media use did not predict depressive symptoms but that depressive symptoms predicted more frequent social media use among adolescent girls. "This is a much more nuanced story," Dennis-Tiwary says. "We know that problematic smartphone use may as likely be a result of mental health problems as a cause, and that calls for a different set of solutions."

Correlational studies have their uses, just as epidemiological research can suggest a link between pollution and increased cancer rates when a randomized clinical trial is not possible. While he thinks it is important not to overstate findings, economist Matthew Gentzkow of Stanford, who studies social media, says of Twenge's work that "there are some pretty striking facts there. They don't tell us whether smartphones are causing mental health problems, but they really shine some light on that possibility. What we need now is to dig in and try to do more careful studies to isolate what's really going on."

A Two-Way Street?

That is what the newest studies set out to do. Hancock's meta-analysis highlighted the fact that many studies on social media and psychological well-being did not measure the same outcomes. Effects generally fell into one of six categories. Three concern positive indicators of well-being: eudaemonic happiness (having a sense of meaning), hedonic happiness (joy in the moment) and relationships. And three are negative: depression, anxiety and loneliness. Hancock and his team found that more social media use was associated slightly with higher depression and anxiety (though not loneliness) and more strongly associated with relationship benefits (though not eudaemonic or hedonic well-being). (The largest effect, at 0.20, was the benefit of stronger relationships.) He and his colleagues also found that active rather than passive use was positively associated with well-being. (They found no effect for passive use, although others have found it to be negative.)

And how researchers asked questions mattered. Framing questions around "addiction" rather than more neutrally makes a negative finding more likely. In all the literature, there were only 24 longitudinal studies, the "gold standard" that allows researchers to compare the relation between well-being and social media use at two points in time and statistically assess which variable is driving change in the other. In these, Hancock's team found a further small but interesting result. "When you have higher well-being, you use social media less, which suggests that well-being is driving [how much use is made of] social media to some degree," Hancock says.

In a trilogy of papers about adolescent technology use, Orben and Przybylski tackled three major pitfalls they had identified in previous analyses of large-scale data sets. The first paper, published in January in *Nature Human Behaviour*, provided both context and a method for improving transparency. It included three data sets from the U.S. and Europe made up of more than 350,000 adolescents. Such data sets are valuable but make it easy to turn up statistically significant results that may not be of practical significance. Przybylski and Orben calculated that if they had followed standard statistical operating procedure, they could have produced roughly 10,000 papers showing negative screen effects, 5,000 indicating no effect and another 4,000 demonstrating positive technology effects on young people—all from the same data sets.

For their new analysis, they used a technique called specification curve analysis, a tool that examines the full range of possible correlations at once. It is the statistical equivalent of seeing the forest for the trees. Analyzed in this way, digital technology use was associated with only 0.4 percent of the variation in adolescent well-being. The wealth of information in the data allowed for the telling comparisons with potatoes and glasses. It also revealed that smoking marijuana and bullying had much larger negative associations for well-being (at 2.7 and 4.3 times worse, respectively, than the average in one of the data sets), whereas positive behaviors such as getting enough sleep and regularly eating breakfast were much more strongly linked to well-being than technology use. "We're trying to move from this mindset of cherry-picking one result to a more holistic picture," Przybylski says. "A key part of that is being able to put these extremely minuscule effects of screens on young people in a real-world context." (Twenge and others question the usefulness of explaining percentages of variation and say it will always turn up small numbers that might mask practical effects.)

Their second paper, published in April in *Psychological Science*, included stronger methods for measuring screen time. They used three data sets from the U.S., the U.K. and Ireland that included time-use diaries in addition to self-reported media usage and measures of well-being. Over a period of five years the more than 17,000 teenagers in the studies were given a diary one day each year. They filled in 10- to 15-minute windows all day long about exactly what they were doing, including use of digital technologies. When Orben and Przybylski applied their statistical technique to the data, there was little evidence for substantial negative associations between digital engagement and well-being. The diaries also allowed them to look at when during the day adolescents were using digital media, including before bed. Even that did not make a difference in well-being, although they did not look at hours of sleep as an outcome, only more general psychological measures.

And finally, in May, with psychologist Tobias Dienlin of the University of Hohenheim in Germany, Orben and Przybylski published a paper in the *Proceedings of the National Academy of Sciences USA*, incorporating longitudinal data to analyze the effect of social media on adolescents' life satisfaction over time. This approach allowed them to ask whether adolescents who are on social media more in a given year than average feel better or worse at year's end and whether feeling better or worse than normal changes social media use in the coming year. Here, too, the result was small and nuanced. "The change in social media use in one year only predicts about 0.25 percent of the variance in the change in life satisfaction over one year," Orben says. "We're talking about fractions of 1 percent changes." The researchers did, however, see slightly stronger effects in girls than in boys, a finding Orben intends to investigate further. The question of individual risk will also be important. "We really want to see if there are reproducible profiles of young people who are more or less vulnerable or resilient to different forms of technology," Przybylski says.

What About Generation Z?

Teenage media use has been a particular concern because of the ubiquity of smartphones today and because adolescence is such a formative period of development. In choosing what to worry about, parents have followed scientists' lead, says psychologist Candice Odgers of the University of California, Irvine. They worry mainly about how much time their children spend online without giving equal attention to the critical question of what they are doing there. Odgers's own work suggests that amount of use is not the problem. In a study published online this summer in *Clinical Psychological Science*, Odgers, Michaeline Jensen of the University of North Carolina at Greensboro and their colleagues followed nearly 400 adolescents for two weeks, sending questions to the teenagers' cell phones three times a day. The study design allowed them to compare mental health symptoms and technology immersion daily as well as over the weeks of the study.

Was media use associated with individual adolescents' well-being? The answer was not really. Routines in place at the start did not predict later mental health symptoms, and mental health was not worse on days teenagers reported spending more or less time on technology.

"It's ironic that in the end the real danger is not smartphones–it's the level of misinformation that's being directed at the public and at parents," Odgers says. "It's consuming so much of the airtime that it's causing us to miss potentially some of the real threats and problems around digital spaces." For her part, Odgers is far more worried about privacy and unequal access to technology for kids from families with lower socioeconomic status. She also suspects that some adolescents find much needed social support online and that adults should pay closer attention to what works in that regard.

Social Media 2.0

These studies are just the beginning. They have helped clarify the big picture on social media usage, but far more work is needed. Variety in the types of studies conducted will help tease out nuance. In a recent experimental study, for instance, Stanford's Gentzkow asked more than 1,600 people to deactivate their Facebook accounts, which was verified electronically. He and his colleagues were surprised that substitution of other digital technologies went down, not up. "People perceive they're spending less time on all these things," Gentzkow says. The effect size was small, however, and masked a lot of individual variation. Some people loved the break; others really missed their online social world. "Facebook is delivering a lot of value to people, but nevertheless they may be using it more than is really optimal for them," Gentzkow says. "There are many people for whom scaling back their usage a little could make them happier and better off."

Several researchers are trying to better measure screen time. Stanford communications researcher Byron Reeves and his colleagues have developed a technique called Screenomics, which takes a picture of people's phones every five seconds (with permission). Technology companies also have a role to play. Corporations are better able than scientists to count how much time individuals are spending on different activities, but they consider that information proprietary, and there are privacy concerns for users to be addressed. Przybylski is pushing for that policy to change. "Companies shouldn't get a free pass," he says.

New research also seeks to do a better job of predicting individual variation. In Hancock's lab, Stanford undergraduate Angela Lee developed a creative approach. She applied the idea of mindsets–that beliefs shape people's realities–to social media. Through interviews, Lee found that views about social media fell into two general buckets: whether someone thought social media was good or bad for them (valence) and whether or not they thought they were in control of it (agency). Over the course of three studies, she and Hancock tested close to 700 people and found that social media mindsets predicted users' well-being. A sense of agency had the strongest effect. "The more you believe you are in control over your social media, the more social support you have, the less depression you report, the less stress, the less social anxiety, regardless of how much you're actually saying you use social media," says Lee, who is now a graduate student in Hancock's lab. She presented the work in May at the Association for Psychological Science meeting.

The power of mindset serves as a reminder of the power of perspective. In the 1980s people were wringing their hands about the time kids spent staring mindlessly at television screens, says Gentzkow, who has studied that era. He imagines asking those worrywarts about new technologies that would allow kids to instead interact with one another by sharing messages, photographs and videos. "Anybody then would have said, 'Wow, that would be amazing.'"

About the Author

Lydia Denworth is a Brooklyn, N.Y.–based science writer and a contributing editor for Scientific American. *She wrote about the neuroscience of stuttering in our August 2021 issue. She is co-author of* Parent Nation.

6 Reasons Smartphones Won't Replace Our Brains

By David Pogue

In my *Scientific American* column this month, I noted that there's not much need to memorize anything anymore. Ask a high-schooler today to rattle off the presidents, the periodic table or state capitals, and you'll get a blank stare—or a "Sure, let me grab my phone." Google is always available. And when's the last time you had to memorize a phone number?

But we'll never consult our phones for everything. Some things are so important we'll have to commit them to memory even if we reach the age of universal digital retrieval. Here are a few of the life categories where memory will always beat digital lookups:

- **The Frequency Factor:** You access some details so often, memorization is required simply because the sheer quantity of lookups would make your life grind to a halt. Spelling, for example. Looking up every word—or directions to work each day or your school locker combination—would do a real number on your productivity.
- **The Cultural Factor:** You can't function for long in society without some basic grounding in history and culture. Without knowing these references you won't have the context to comprehend current events—or even know what you're missing or what questions to ask. You won't understand advertisements, editorials or even news articles. And you won't get anybody's jokes. You'll be unemployable and undatable.
- **The Social Factor:** You'll always have to know basic facts about your friends and family (and, of course, yourself). You should have instant access to your boss's name, your spouse's birthday and the names of your best friend's children. Fumbling to look them up electronically in a face-to-face situation would result in a lot of hurt feelings (and possibly unemployment).

- **The Security Factor:** Clearly, our gadgets can go a long way toward eliminating the need to memorize passwords. Programs like Dashlane and LastPass autofill our login information on the Web sites we visit, and even fill in our credit card information when we buy something online. But you still have to unlock those programs each day by entering a master password–one you'll have to memorize. That's true of physical security, too: you can automate parts of it, but at the end of the line, there's a physical key or card or fob. You have to know where to find it and how to use it.
- **The Productivity Factor:** Even if your daily work requires something you could easily look up, like molecular weights, stock symbols or commonly prescribed drugs, your work would bog down to a halt if you had to interrupt your flow every few minutes for a lookup. You need fluency in your own career facts to operate effectively.
- **The Lookup Factor:** Our gadgets may always be able to call up information on demand–but only if you know how and where to look for it. You still have to know how to use the tools of modern up-lookings: like Rotten Tomatoes, Wikipedia, Dictionary.com or–What's the other one? Oh, yeah–Google.

About the Author

David Pogue is the anchor columnist for Yahoo Tech and host of several NOVA miniseries on PBS.

Generation Z: Online and at Risk?

By Nicholas Kardaras

"I'm going to kill you while you are both asleep," the wild-eyed 13-year-old girl said as she flailed and kicked her father before biting his arm. This was the second time in less than a week that "Heidi" had flown into a violent rage because her parents had taken away her Chromebook and her access to social media. It would also be the second time that she would have to be taken to the psychiatric emergency room.

When her parents, "John" and "Melanie," first called me for help, they described Heidi as a sweet, happy, loving girl whose teachers had always declared their favorite student. With a tendency to gravitate toward overachievers, she loved playing soccer, hiking and taking mountain bike rides with her dad–the man she bit.

John and Melanie, supportive suburban New Jersey parents with college degrees and their own tech business, were blindsided by Heidi's social media addiction. "It all started when she came home in seventh grade with a Chromebook that the school had given her," they told me. Ostensibly given for school purposes, the Chromebook came loaded with Google Classroom–which also, unfortunately, included Google Chat and various Google Chat communities.

Once this educational Trojan horse entered their home, John and Melanie found that Heidi was more and more preoccupied with its social media chat rooms, spending hours on them every night. Because the chat rooms were part of the Chromebook platform, they were not able to disable them. Then Heidi started becoming preoccupied with raunchy YouTube videos and also began playing Squarelaxy, an addictive progression game similar to Minecraft, which allowed her to be online with other Squarelaxy players.

Over the course of a year John and Melanie saw their daughter transform from a sweet, innocent girl who loved spending time with her parents into a sexualized, foul-mouthed and violent terror. And sadly, she became a girl in need of psychiatric treatment.

Early adolescence is a time of dramatic change for most kids, and arguably, Heidi may have been headed for trouble with or without her Chromebook. It is also true that many kids use social media responsibly and without issue. But a growing body of evidence shows that social media and immersion in the digital world can be contributing factors in the development of an array of psychological problems–from addiction to depression–and young people may be especially vulnerable.

A Perfect Storm

Social connection is not only the most essential part of being human, it is also a key ingredient in happiness and health. Thanks to social media, we are the most connected society that has ever lived: each second people in the U.S. send more than 7,500 tweets, 1,394 Instagram photographs, and two million e-mails; they also view more than 119,000 YouTube videos. We keep texting as if our lives depended on it: As of 2012, Americans sent about 69,000 texts a second, with more than six billion sent every day. Globally, that number is 23 billion daily texts and 8.3 trillion annually.

Predictably, the younger you are, the more you text. According to a 2011 Pew Research Center poll, cell-phone owners between the ages of 18 and 24 send or receive an average of 109.5 messages on a normal day, whereas all adults (18 and older) exchange a daily average of 41.5 messages, with a median of only 10 texts daily. As for social media, a 2015 report compiled by the marketing agency We Are Social estimated that more than two billion people–over a quarter of the world's population–have active social media accounts.

For a species hardwired for social connection, that should be a wonderful thing. And yet the rise of social media and technology has coincided with an apparent decline in mental health. In 2014 psychologist Jean M. Twenge of San Diego State University analyzed data from nearly seven million teenagers and adults across the U.S. and found that more people reported symptoms of depression in recent years than they did in the 1980s. Teens, in particular, are now 74 percent more likely to have trouble sleeping and twice as likely to see a professional for mental health issues. According to a 2016 fact sheet from the World Health Organization, depression is now the leading cause of disability globally, affecting 350 million people worldwide.

There are certainly many intervening factors that may be driving this global trend, but we do have preliminary research linking depression with social media usage. In 2014 Mai-Ly Steers of the University of Houston and her colleagues surveyed 180 college students and found that the more time these subjects spent on Facebook, the more likely they were to experience mild depressive symptoms. The researchers attributed the link to the psychological phenomenon known as social comparison–and comparing our lives to others can seem particularly harsh online, where people tend to post only the highlights. In a 2014 study, social psychologists Christina Sagioglou and Tobias Greitemeyer, both at the University of Innsbruck in Austria, found another reason why people can feel down after Facebook sessions: they feel that the time spent is not meaningful.

In addition, online socializing may be interfering with our face-to-face encounters. That is troubling because we know that we can get physically and psychologically ill without real human contact. Indeed, several studies have shown that people can go insane if cut off from human interaction. The reason is that, as social creatures, we find purpose and meaning and bolster our emotional states largely through the social and cultural context created by contact with others. Not getting the right kind of human contact and nurturing support at key developmental periods in childhood can lead to profound emotional and psychological problems.

Social media has an impact on other basic psychological needs–including our need for novelty, called neophilia. As writer Winifred Gallagher points out in *New: Understanding Our Need for Novelty and Change*, our human brain is biologically primed for novelty, which, in turn, has helped us to survive cataclysmic environmental change. Unfortunately, this hardwired thirst can be overwhelming in the information age, in which every hyperlink, tweet, text, e-mail and Instagram photograph can be an opportunity to experience something new. As with an alcoholic in a liquor store or a chocolate lover at Willy Wonka's, the multitude of opportunities for novelty can be exhaustingly hyperstimulating.

And what about the human need to experience reward? We know that humans like activities that release the neurotransmitter dopamine in the brain—a lot. Evolution has given us incentives via a "dopamine tickle" to pursue certain life-sustaining activities, such as eating and sex, because dopamine made us feel good. But we have discovered that digital stimulation feels pretty good, too, and similarly lights up our dopamine-reward pathways.

So then where does modern digital technology, which plays off these intersecting human needs for connection, reward and novelty, leave us? Short answer: addicted or, at the very least, potentially vulnerable to screen addiction. Many adults and kids have developed compulsive texting and social media habits precisely because such predilections quench our thirst for novelty while tickling our dopamine-reward pathways. And like addicts, they can go into withdrawal without it.

Teenage Hypertexting

In 2010 journalism professor Susan Moeller and her colleagues at the University of Maryland asked 200 students to give up all media, including texting, for 24 hours. Many showed signs of withdrawal, craving and anxiety. "Texting and IM'ing my friends gives me a constant feeling of comfort," one student said. "When I did not have those two luxuries, I felt quite alone and secluded in my life." Another put it in even more direct terms: "I clearly am addicted, and the dependency is sickening." According to a 2015 study of millennial communication habits by psychologist Kelly Lister-Landman, now at Delaware County Community College, and her colleagues, "text messaging has increased dramatically among adolescents over the past 10 years," and many teenage texters share addictlike symptoms and behaviors. In fact, the researchers indicated that such teens have a lot in common with compulsive gamblers, including lost sleep because of the activity, problems cutting back and a tendency to lie to cover up the amount of time they spend doing it.

The study clarified that the frequency of texting does not by itself equate to compulsion. The key is its effect on a person and his or her life. As Lister-Landman explained in a press release: "Compulsive texting ... involves trying and failing to cut back on texting, becoming defensive when challenged about the behavior, and feeling frustrated when one can't do it." Based on those criteria, although boys texted with the same frequency as girls, the study determined that girls were four times more likely to have texting-related problems.

Perhaps even more shocking, a 2012 Pew survey by researcher Amanda Lenhart–which involved a nationally representative sample of 799 12- to 17-year-olds–found that only 35 percent said they regularly socialized face-to-face anymore, compared with a whopping 63 percent of teens who said they communicated mostly via text messages and averaged 167 texts a day.

Beyond addictive tendencies and an erosion of face-to-face socialization, Lister-Landman and her colleagues also found a link between compulsive texting and poor academic behavior. And a 2010 research study at the Case Western Reserve University School of Medicine that looked at the texting habits of 4,257 high school students revealed that 20 percent of those teens engaged in hypertexting, or sending more than 120 daily texts; these hypertexters were twice as likely to have tried alcohol, 41 percent more likely to have used illegal drugs, nearly three and a half times more likely to have had sex, and 90 percent more likely to have had four or more sex partners.

What are we to make of all of these statistics that link more texting with more behavioral problems? I would look at these data a couple of different ways. First of all, if a person is a compulsive or addicted texter, it indicates to me that he or she has an impulse-control problem. People who have a harder time controlling their impulses also naturally tend to be more impulsive in other areas of their lives: trying drugs, drinking excessively, having sex. But here we also have the age-old chicken-or-egg question: Are people who are impulsive to start with gravitating toward digital excess, or is the digital excess creating or reinforcing the impulsivity? Possibly both.

We can also view problematic behavior linked to excessive social media usage through another lens. According to social learning theory, we model our behavior after our peers. What if I have hundreds of peers who text and use social media? I then increase the likelihood of getting exposed to certain problematic behavior. For example, if I hang out with five kids, and one of them smokes marijuana and has multiple sex partners, the influence on my own behavior might be minimal. Now, through social media, I am hanging out with several hundred kids–and what if 30 or 40 of them have multiple sex partners? Or are taking Vicodin or Xanax? The impact of that larger–and potentially more troublesome–group on my own behavior is now greater.

The Illusion of Real Connection

Apart from the addictive nature of our new digital way of connecting, it does not seem to satisfy our deep-seated need for true human contact. Instead what it seems to have spawned is the illusion of social connection via a medium that has our dopamine receptors on perpetual high alert as we anticipate, like Pavlovian dogs, the next "ping" that promises to offer us the novelty and pleasure of a text, instant message, tweet, Facebook update or Instagram photograph.

More than two decades ago anthropologist and evolutionary psychologist Robin Dunbar, now at the University of Oxford, proposed the theory that a person can maintain about 150 acquaintances but only five or so close relationships–our brain cannot handle more. The figure of 150, also known as Dunbar's number, was, as he put it, a measurement of the "cognitive limit to the number of individuals with whom any one person can maintain stable relationships." Amazingly, Dunbar discovered that these numbers have remained more or less constant throughout history.

Social media has not really affected this dynamic. When data scientist Bruno Gonçalves and his colleagues, all then at Indiana University Bloomington, looked at whether Twitter had changed the number of relationships that users could maintain, they found that people could still manage to follow between 100 and 200 stable connections. But the Dunbar number represents a continuum, with the most intimate, and perhaps most important, figure being five, or the number of truly close friends whom we see often and call in serious situations.

Researchers have attributed the benefits of these face-to-face relationships to the "shared experience" effect: when you laugh or cry with someone, when you go to a social event or have dinner together, when you experience life together, there is a deepening of the social bond that cannot be replicated by social media. In social media, you can "share" and "like" something with your Facebook friends, or you can watch the same hysterical YouTube clip of a dancing chimp, but it is not the same as if you had done something together.

There may also be a physiological aspect of friendship that Facebook friends can never replace. Over the past several years Dunbar and his colleagues have been looking at the importance of physical contact. He already knew that in primate grooming, touch activates the endorphin system; now we know that the same is true for humans. In a series of studies, Dunbar and his colleagues showed that light touch triggers an endorphin response that is important for creating a personal bond. According to Dunbar, our skin has a set of neurons, common to all mammals, that respond to light stroking but not to any other kind of touch.

"We think that's what they exist for, to trigger endorphin responses as a consequence of grooming," Dunbar explained in an interview with the *New Yorker*. Just as dopamine incentivizes eating and procreating, it seems that endorphins released with physical touch encourage human bonding. Facebook friends just cannot replicate that; they cannot pat us on the back, rub our knees or give us hugs.

Dunbar is also concerned about the negative developmental effect that our new digital world will have on children. From past research on social interaction, we know that early childhood experiences are crucial in developing those parts of the brain that are dedicated to social interaction, empathy and other interpersonal skills. If we deprive children of interaction and touch early on because they mostly socially interact via screens, those brain areas may not fully develop.

Facebook Depression

What would such a "glow kid"–raised on mostly digital social interactions–look like as an older person? "This is the big imponderable. We haven't yet seen an entire generation that's grown up with things like Facebook go through adulthood yet," Dunbar said in the same *New Yorker* interview. "It's quite conceivable that we might end up less social in the future, which would be a disaster because we need to be more social–our world has become so large." What then happens to a person–particularly a kid–who does not have those real-life connections and is already feeling a bit alienated and sad? In those instances, the illusion of connection created by social media may actually do more harm than good.

Consider the phenomenon known as Facebook depression, whereby the more "friends" one has on Facebook, the higher the likelihood of depression. There is also, as mentioned, the double whammy that the more time spent on social media and the more texting a person does, the higher the likelihood of not just depression but tech addiction as well. While it is hard to say which way the causality goes (does depression drive more time on social media or the other way around, or both?), this much is clear: more screen time only further amplifies the isolation and disconnection from healthier activities and meaningful face-to-face social contact.

The previously mentioned Case Western hypertexting study also looked at "hypernetworking"–defined as more than three hours per school day on social networking sites. The 11.5 percent of students who met the criteria were subject to higher rates of depression, substance abuse, poor sleep, stress, poor academic performance and suicide. Perhaps not so shockingly, hypernetworkers were also found to have more permissive parents. Just as the hypertexting kids engaged in more risky behavior, hypernetworking teens were also found to be 69 percent more likely to have tried sex, 60 percent more likely to report four or more sexual partners, 84 percent more likely to have used illegal drugs and 94 percent more likely to have been in a physical fight.

"This should be a wake-up call for parents," warned the study's lead researcher, epidemiologist Scott Frank, in a Case Western press release. They should "not only help their children stay safe by not texting and driving, but by discouraging excessive use of the cell phone or social websites in general."

I think that most reasonable people can understand that texting as a way to communicate and social media as a way to stay connected both have a place in our society. But if you want healthy and happy kids, it is vitally important that they have supportive, caring relationships with flesh-and-blood people. If they must have Facebook accounts or phones with texting capability—although some parents now opt for nontexting "dumb" phones—at least wait until the children are far enough along developmentally that they are less vulnerable to tech addiction, Facebook depression or hypertexting. Even then, the research shows that monitoring your child's digital habits and virtual friends is critical in the new social media and texting landscape.

About the Author

Nicholas Kardaras is executive director of the Dunes East Hampton in New York State, where he treats clients with addiction and mental health issues.

Media Multitasking Disrupts Memory, Even in Young Adults

By Bret Stetka

The bulky, modern human brain evolved hundreds of thousands of years ago and, for the most part, has remained largely unchanged. That is, it is innately tuned to analog information–to focus on the hunt at hand or perhaps the forage for wild plants. Yet we now pummel our ancient thinking organ with a daily deluge of digital information that many scientists believe may have enduring and worrisome effects.

A new study published today in *Nature* supports the concern. The research suggests that "media multitasking"–or engaging with multiple forms of digital or screen-based media simultaneously, whether they are television, texting or Instagram–may impair attention in young adults, worsening their ability to later recall specific situations or experiences.

The authors of the new paper used electroencephalography–a technique that measures brain activity–and eye tracking to assess attention in 80 young adults between the ages of 18 and 26. The study participants were first presented with images of objects on a computer screen and asked to classify the pleasantness or size of each one. After a 10-minute break, the subjects were then shown additional objects and asked whether they were already classified or new. By analyzing these individuals' brain and eye responses as they were tasked with remembering, the researchers could identify the number of lapses in their attention. These findings were then compared to the results of a questionnaire the participants were asked to fill out that quantified everyday attention, mind wandering and media multitasking.

Higher reported media multitasking correlated with a tendency toward attentional lapses and decreased pupil diameter, a known marker of reduced attention. And attention gaps just prior to remembering were linked with forgetting the earlier images and reduced brain-signal patterns known to be associated with episodic memory–the recall of particular events.

Previous work had shown a connection between media multitasking and poorer episodic memory. The new findings offer clues as to why this might be the case. "We found evidence that one's ability to sustain attention helps to explain the relationship between heavier media multitasking and worse memory," says the paper's lead author Kevin Madore, a postdoctoral fellow in the department of psychology at Stanford University. "Individuals who are heavier media multitaskers may also show worse memory because they have lower sustained attention ability."

"This is an impressive study," comments Daphne Bavelier, a professor of psychology at the University of Geneva in Switzerland, who was not involved in the new research. "The work is important as it identifies a source of interindividual variability when one is cued to remember information"–the differences in attention among the study participants. "These findings are novel and tell us something important about the relationship between attention and memory, and their link to everyday behavior ..., [something] we did not know before," adds Harvard University psychologist Daniel L. Schacter, who was also not involved in the study.

Madore points out that the new findings are, for now, correlational. They do not indicate if media multitasking leads to impaired attention or if people with worse attention and memory are just more prone to digital distractions. They also do not necessarily implicate any specific media source as detrimental to the brain. As work by Bavelier found, action video games in particular harbor plenty of potential for improving brain function.

But Madore and his colleagues, including senior author of the paper and Stanford psychologist Anthony D. Wagner, hope to clarify these unknowns in future studies. They also hope to pursue attention-training interventions that could help improve attention and memory in people prone to distraction.

With winter looming and the COVID-19 pandemic keeping us indoors, Madore feels the new study stresses the need to be mindful of how we engage with media. "I think our data point to the importance of being consciously aware of attentiveness," he says, whether that awareness means resisting media multitasking during school lectures or work Zoom sessions or making sure not to idly flip through your Facebook feed while half watching the new Borat movie.

About the Author

Bret Stetka is a writer based in New York City and editorial director of Medscape Neurology (a subsidiary of WebMD). His work has appeared in Wired*, on NPR and in the* Atlantic*. He graduated from the University of Virginia School of Medicine in 2005.*

How GPS Weakens Memory—and What We Can Do About It

By Mar Gonzalez-Franco, Gregory Dane Clemenson and Amos Miller

Using mobile phones to navigate has become second nature. Whether you're heading to a new park, meeting friends at a restaurant, or going to run errands, you just tap the location on your phone and go. Prior to GPS, exploring and wayfinding in new places required preparation. We had to think, consult paper maps, and plan and memorize parts of our route. But in today's technological world, there is no need to think. Simply follow the turn-by-turn directions on your phone, and you'll end up where you need to be. But your overall sense of the place suffers. Spatial navigation, which had been a process performed exclusively by the human brain and perceptual system, has now been surrendered to technology.

However, in doing so, we also surrendered our agency. Does it matter?

There are structures in the brain dedicated to these complex pathfinding tasks. In particular, the hippocampus is deeply associated with supporting spatial memory, spatial navigation and mental mapping.

Anthropologists have gone so far as to suggest that navigation needs might have been the starting point for all memories (as discussed in Nicholas Carr's book *The Glass Cage*). For example, mnemonic techniques for remembering large numbers such as the digits of pi often rely on the "memory palace" (or "method of loci") made famous by Cicero, with multiple floors and connected chambers in which one mentally stores the digits. One can then recall a long sequence of digits through an imaginary navigation, revisiting the chambers of this memory palace.

If We Don't Use It, We Lose It

As we age, our memory declines. And while there is no silver bullet for healthy aging, neuroscientists agree that one of the key ingredients of successful aging is staying mentally active. Studies show that we can actually exercise the hippocampus memory through exploration and spatial navigation. Expert navigators such as London cab drivers have larger hippocampi compared to regular populations in consequence of their intensive spatial mapping and multisensory experience of the city.

If spatial navigation is such an essential element to healthy aging and mental activity, why surrender this critical skill to our phones? By following a set of digital turn-by-turn directions, GPS navigation apps treat us as passive passengers rather than active explorers, removing our agency to make decisions. In turn this inhibits our ability to create proper mental maps of the surrounding environment, and negatively impacts the hippocampus, which is critical for brain health.

While advances in technology clearly have many benefits, we must remain mindful that technology can influence the brain. Ultimately our goal should be to create and design technology in ways that complement our brain and enhance our opportunities to interact and engage with the real world around us.

Physical Maps, the First Revolution

Mental maps arise from direct experience. As we explore new environments, the brain constantly maps out our surroundings. And we use all of our senses to learn about and remember our surroundings, not just vision. In particular, evolution rewarded auditory navigation: as hunter-gatherers we listened to the environment and moved towards sounds, allowing us to avoid predators, track prey and locate water sources. Our brains ultimately could generate detailed maps of our environment through active exploration, a hard-won evolutionary skill that never went away.

So even today, strolling along a modern city waterfront, we might hear the petulant squawks of seagulls fighting over a bread crust, or the low throaty notes of approaching ships in the fog. We refer to such distinctive, spatially situated sounds as auditory beacons.

However, as civilizations expanded and grew, it became more difficult to navigate over long distances only through sensory experiences and memory. One cannot sail to another continent on senses alone. So, maps were a revolution for humanity. Rudimentary maps were created as early as 16,500 B.C. when people drew paintings on the walls of caves showing stars or landscape features. Later, these were carved into wood or rocks so they could be carried while traveling. But it wasn't until the ancient Greeks and early Chinese dynasties that the first paper maps appeared.

Physical maps were a revolution. They can contain enormous amounts of information about the surrounding environment on a simple piece of paper, but using them successfully requires both the correct placement of oneself within the map and the correct heading. Maps are an example of allocentric navigation, with allo- meaning "other": all the information on the map is displayed as it relates to other features and landmarks within the environment.

In contrast, a set of directions is direct and easy to follow. Directions are an example of egocentric navigation, with ego- meaning "self": all information is relative to the person's current position and orientation. However, egocentric navigation and directions are considerably less flexible as they only work from a single location and contain significantly less information about the broader environment.

The challenge is that physical maps can be very abstract and require many other techniques to operate, such as the ability to determine where in the map one is located. Indeed, maps evolved in parallel with wayfinding techniques. Wayfinding tools empower self-location, from compass to stars, latitude, longitude and realigning landmarks. Such tools allow us to achieve the self-location and heading necessary for allocentric navigation. But the expertise needed to be a successful navigator is not within everyone's grasp. Even commercial airplanes used to have an expert navigator on board: a person dedicated to determining the aircraft's current position–and next changes to heading–on top of a map. At the individual level most of us didn't have the luxury to afford a navigator, and families would have table discussions preparing routes for their trips. And then assign their own familial navigators.

GPS Navigation

The rise of satellite-enabled GPS was revolutionary for navigation, and with the rise of mobile phones, anyone can have their personal navigator. We can go places spontaneously, with little need for planning or additional people to navigate. GPS navigation apps enable egocentric navigation with easy-to-follow turn-by-turn directions: "Turn right in 100 meters, then turn left," all the way to the destination. With these conveniences at our fingertips, we are no longer active navigators; we are passive passengers aboard the GPS.

However, multiple experiments have shown that this easy egocentric navigation also reduces spatial awareness and mental mapping when compared to more traditional forms of allocentric navigation like paper maps. See for example recent work by Eran Ben-Elia comparing paper maps to Google Maps, in which app users significantly underperformed on traditional memory map tasks such as pointing or landmark recognition.

Our question is: Can we find a way to still use GPS but reduce the harmful effects of current GPS navigation on memory?

The challenge is to create alternative forms of GPS navigation that will remain easy enough for the general public, but also enable allocentric navigation and thus be more likely to improve spatial awareness.

Our research finds that appropriately designed audio beacons offer an alternative that fosters a much more active form of egocentric navigation. Instead of guiding users to turn right and turn left on the way to their desired destination, we can convert a location of interest to a distinctive auditory beacon (digital versions of the aforementioned petulant squawks and low throaty notes) via earbuds or headphones. Our auditory navigation application, known as Soundscape, has an effect that resembles a church bell or minaret, where peals or calls to prayer can be heard at great distance; our would-be navigator can make way by heading toward the sound.

But audio beacons can be created for any chosen destination, and without sound decay, so they can be heard from as far away as needed. With an audio beacon at the destination, a pharmacy two miles away can produce a sound that we can hear through our phone. Then one simply moves towards it, but unlike with turn-by-turn directions, you can build spatial awareness through active and direct exploration of the environment along the way.

In recent experiments, available in our publication in *Scientific Reports* (an open-access journal by the publisher of *Nature*), we show that this type of sensory navigation through audio beacons outperforms turn-by-turn navigation in the creation of mental maps.

We believe these results, at least in part, derive from people taking a more active role in their navigation. They explore more while using auditory beacons, and can engage with the environment, both of which support allocentric navigation and the construction of mental maps.

We invite the reader to try such auditory beacon experience by trying the Soundscape app on their mobile phone. The Soundscape team originally designed the app as an experimental tool to enable blind and low vision populations with a potentially safer, more robust and accessible navigation than turn-by-turn options; to date, it has enabled over 500,000 walks in seven countries.

Auditory beacon navigation is an example of how we are entering into an era where noxious effects of automation on our brain health will be at the forefront of technological development. Technology does not need to replace our evolutionary functions and distance us from our environments, but rather with appropriate design can complement the sensory inputs processed by our brain. In that regard, GPS navigation based on auditory beacons offers a compelling example of a sensory augmentation that helps humans connect more deeply with reality; perhaps instead of evolving into a new species of turn-by-turn zombies, we can thereby all engage more deeply with humanity, our local environment, and life itself.

This is an opinion and analysis article.

About the Authors

Mar Gonzalez-Franco, Ph.D., is a neuroscientist and computer scientist at Microsoft Research. Her work is at the intersection of human perception and computer science. In her research, she fosters new forms of interaction that will revolutionize how humans use technologies. Her interest lies in spatial computing and on the wild use of technology. Follow her on Twitter @twi_mar.

Gregory Dane Clemenson, Ph.D., is a neuroscientist at the University of California, Irvine, specializing in spatial navigation and memory. His research has evolved from studying the effects of Alzheimer's in rats to exploring the impact of technology on the human brain, the latter a field in which he has taken a pioneering role.

Amos Miller is the leader of Microsoft Soundscape, a project by the Microsoft Research Enable team. His interest is in technologies that augment human perception and sensory interaction with the environment and that promote inclusive experiences for people with different abilities. He also happens to be blind and has been creating Soundscape to empower all people to be able to navigate through the world freely like never before.

Your Brain on Google Maps

By Zeynep Tufekci

More than a billion people around the world have smartphones, almost all of which come with some kind of navigation app such as Google or Apple Maps or Waze. This raises the age-old question we encounter with any technology: What skills are we losing? But also, crucially: What capabilities are we gaining?

Talking with people who are good at finding their way around or adept at using paper maps, I often hear a lot of frustration with digital maps. North/south orientation gets messed up, and you can see only a small section at a time. And unlike with paper maps, one loses a lot of detail after zooming out.

I can see all that and sympathize that it may be quite frustrating for the already skilled to be confined to a small phone screen. (Although map apps aren't really meant to be replacements for paper maps, which appeal to our eyes, but are actually designed to be heard: "Turn left in 200 feet. Your destination will be on the right.")

But consider what digital navigation aids have meant for someone like me. Despite being a frequent traveler, I'm so terrible at finding my way that I still use Google Maps almost every day in the small town where I have lived for many years. What looks like an inferior product to some has been a significant expansion of my own capabilities. I'd even call it life-changing.

Part of the problem is that reading paper maps requires a specific skill set. There is nothing natural about them. In many developed nations, including the U.S., one expects street names and house numbers to be meaningful referents, and instructions such as "go north for three blocks and then west" make sense to those familiar with these conventions. In Istanbul, in contrast, where I grew up, none of those hold true. For one thing, the locals rarely use street names. Why bother when a government or a military coup might change them–again. House and apartment numbers often aren't sequential either because after buildings 1, 2 and 3 were built, someone squeezed in another house between 1 and 2, and now that's 4. But then 5 will maybe get built after 3, and 6 will be between 2 and 3. Good luck with 1, 4, 2, 6, 5, and so on, sometimes into the hundreds, in jumbled order. Besides, the city is full of winding, ancient alleys that intersect with newer avenues at many angles. Instructions as simple as "go north" would require a helicopter or a bulldozer.

In such places, you navigate by making your way to a large, well-known landmark and asking whomever is around how to get to your destination—which involves getting to the next big landmark and asking again. In American suburbs, however, there is often nobody outside to ask—and even when there is, "turn right at the next ornate mosque" is a different level of specificity than "turn right at the next strip mall."

All of this means that between my arrival in more developed nations and the arrival of Google Maps, I got lost all the time, searching in vain for someone to ask. Even when I traveled to cities that were old like Istanbul, I still felt uncomfortable. I didn't necessarily speak the language well enough or know the major landmarks so my skills didn't transfer.

I tried many techniques, and maybe I would have gotten eventually better—who knows? But along came Google Maps, like a fairy grandmother whispering directions in my ear.

Since then, I travel with a lot more confidence, and my world has opened up. Maybe it is true that I am especially directionally challenged, but I cannot be the only one. And because I go to more places more confidently, I believe my native navigation skills have somewhat improved, too.

Which brings me back to my original question: while we often lose some skills after outsourcing the work to technology, this new setup may also allow us to expand our capabilities. Consider the calculator: I don't doubt that our arithmetic skills might have regressed a bit as the little machines became ubiquitous, but calculations that were once tedious and error-prone are now much more straightforward—and one can certainly do more complex equations more confidently. Maybe when technology closes a door, we should also look for the doors it opens.

About the Author

Zeynep Tufekci is an associate professor at the University of North Carolina, whose research revolves around how technology, science, and society interact.

Tech Dealers Now Trying to Save the Tech "Addicts" They've Created

By Larry Greenemeier

A group of former Silicon Valley insiders recently issued a stark warning to the app-and-update-obsessed public: Social media, the Web, mobile apps and other technologies developed to "monetize our attention" are "now eroding the pillars of our society," according to the Center for Humane Technology. The new organization's goal is to push tech companies to create products that benefit society, rather than simply manipulating people's behavior for profit.

Led by a former Google "design ethicist" as well as former managers at Mozilla (maker of the Firefox Web browser) and chipmaker Nvidia, the center faces several challenges. Foremost among them is the irony that it will have to rely on social media and the Web to reach a large enough audience to have any impact. The group also acknowledges the futility of trying to change the business practices of YouTube, Facebook, Snapchat, Twitter and other companies that make lots of money by grabbing and holding people's attention.

Instead, the organization–which includes a number of entrepreneurs who have already made fortunes helping peddle the possibly addictive technologies in question–will encourage tech companies to design new products that are less distracting and actually reduce the amount of time people spend staring at their screens. Another important aspect of the center's charter is to pressure governments to create greater consumer protections.

Is tech addiction a real condition? If so, how do you know if you're addicted? And is the Center for Humane Technology a potential solution or just another distraction? *Scientific American* posed these and other questions to Simon McCarthy-Jones, an associate professor in the Department of Psychiatry at Trinity College Dublin in Ireland. McCarthy-Jones's most recent book is *Can't You*

Hear Them? The Science and Significance of Hearing Voices; he has also written about the need to weigh the benefits and costs of social networking.

[An edited transcript of the conversation follows.]

Q: At what point does incessant use of technology become an addiction, as opposed to a better way to work or occupy idle time?

A: One way to consider whether tech use crosses over into addiction is to look at the six criteria that Mark Griffiths [a professor of behavioral addiction at Nottingham Trent University in England] has argued need to be met for a behavior to be deemed an addiction. Using social networking sites as an example, are these the overriding focus of your life, dominating your thoughts, feelings and behaviors? Are you using them to cause a specific change in your mood–for example, to induce euphoria or numbing? Do you need to increase your use of them to gain the same level of benefits? If you can't access the site, does this have negative effects on you, such as irritability or headaches? Does your use of the site cause conflict with important people in your life such as your partner, children or employer? And do you continually fall back into your problematic social network use after periods of abstinence or being in control?

If you meet all these criteria, you could be said to have a social networking site addiction, although this is not–yet–a recognized psychiatric disorder. The same approach can be applied to other online activities such as gaming. Indeed, internet gaming disorder is identified in the current edition of the *DSM–5* [*Diagnostic and Statistical Manual of Mental Disorders, Fifth Edition*], psychiatry's bible, as a condition recommended for further study. Gaming disorder has likewise made it into the beta draft of the World Health Organization's forthcoming updated International Classification of Diseases.

Q: Why do so many people obsessively check their devices and social media accounts for updates?

A: We can become addicted to certain tech products because our use of them is reinforced. They can help us fulfill a range of psychological needs such as belonging, status and competence. Using them can be intrinsically motivating, resulting in feelings of competence, excitement or of being "in the zone," each of which has its own reward. Tech can also be extrinsically motivating; its use yields rewards from others, such as approval. Tech products can also help us avoid painful thoughts, feelings and realities. In a society where many people–particularly men–have proved in research experiments that they would rather electrocute themselves than sit in silence with their thoughts, the urge to get away from ourselves should not be underestimated. Also feeding the addictive behavior: Many tech products serve up rewards at unpredictable moments. For example, you never know when a status notification is going to pop up on Facebook. This encourages compulsive use.

Q: What makes someone prone to tech addiction?

A: There are many such reasons, but let's take three as examples. First, your personality influences how prone you might be to tech addiction. A Belgian study found people who used social network sites compulsively were less emotionally stable, less agreeable and less conscientious. Those people also had lower levels of perceived control and self-esteem. And compulsive social network users were more lonely and depressed than people who did not use these sites in this way. Second, there is evidence that possessing genetic variants associated with lower levels of dopamine function make you more likely to use internet video games excessively. And, third, why you are using tech products influences addiction proneness. For example, internet gaming addiction is associated with using such games to try and cope with negative emotions, to connect to people and to [master some skill].

To point this out is not to blame the user. People are exposed to a powerful product designed to draw them in while living in [an actual] culture that at times seems callous and liable to push them away. Any answer to problematic tech use involves product, person and society.

Q: Is there evidence that gadget and social media companies have engineered their technology to be addictive?

A: If someone were trying to design a tech product that was addictive, it would look a lot like many of the products on the market today. Indeed, market forces would appear to encourage the development of addictive tech products. Some companies advertise how their knowledge of mechanisms involved in addiction—such as dopamine release and learning theory—can be used to help other businesses increase their customers' usage and loyalty, albeit potentially for health and other benefits to the customer. So it could look from the outside like some tech products were designed to be addictive. That said, some have argued this may not have been the case.

Q: Can the center's digital campaign address the problem, particularly if the group is trying to reach people through the same technology it condemns?

A: The center seems to be aware of the irony. On their Web site they mention having a Facebook page by writing, "Sigh..., we do have a Facebook group." The site also recommends using something called Newsfeed Eradicator [a Google Chrome browser extension that allows Facebook users to access their messages, notifications and groups, but not their newsfeed]. Nevertheless, I think I might see the issue slightly differently to the way they do. I would raise the question: Are some tech products violating our right to freedom of thought?

Q: How does freedom of thought tie into the center's message?

A: A great article by the international human rights barrister Susie Alegre recently explored the relation between modern technology and the right to freedom of thought. As she notes, if freedom of thought involves the freedom to keep our thoughts private, how will this square with, for example, Facebook's planned brain-computer interface? Alegre also observes that freedom of thought involves freedom from indoctrination or influence through manipulation. If we think of the now infamous 2014 Facebook newsfeed experiment [in which the company purposely manipulated information posted on 689,000 users' home pages] or the claim by Center for Humane Technology co-founder Tristan Harris that tech companies are "shaping the thoughts and feelings and actions of people" and are "programming people," we may wonder if this right is currently being observed.

Given we have an absolute right to freedom of thought, the Center for Humane Technology could consider this in their work. A human-rights based approach, focusing on potential tech violations of the absolute right to freedom of thought, could be a useful additional tactic for them. The center's argument that tech's manipulation of us is unethical suggests the tech should change. In contrast, if it were deemed that tech's manipulation of us violates our absolute right to freedom of thought, this means the tech must change.

About the Author

Larry Greenemeier is the associate editor of technology for Scientific American, *covering a variety of tech-related topics, including biotech, computers, military tech, nanotech, and robots.*

The Reading Brain in the Digital Age: Why Paper Still Beats Screens

By Ferris Jabr

One of the most provocative viral YouTube videos in the past two years begins mundanely enough: a one-year-old girl plays with an iPad, sweeping her fingers across its touch screen and shuffling groups of icons. In following scenes, she appears to pinch, swipe and prod the pages of paper magazines as though they, too, are screens. Melodramatically, the video replays these gestures in close-up.

For the girl's father, the video–*A Magazine Is an iPad That Does Not Work*–is evidence of a generational transition. In an accompanying description, he writes, "Magazines are now useless and impossible to understand, for digital natives"–that is, for people who have been interacting with digital technologies from a very early age, surrounded not only by paper books and magazines but also by smartphones, Kindles and iPads.

Whether or not his daughter truly expected the magazines to behave like an iPad, the video brings into focus a question that is relevant to far more than the youngest among us: How exactly does the technology we use to read change the way we read?

Since at least the 1980s researchers in psychology, computer engineering, and library and information science have published more than 100 studies exploring differences in how people read on paper and on screens. Before 1992 most experiments concluded that people read stories and articles on screens more slowly and remember less about them. As the resolution of screens on all kinds of devices sharpened, however, a more mixed set of findings began to emerge. Recent surveys suggest that although most people still prefer paper–especially when they need to concentrate for a long time–attitudes are changing as tablets and e-reading technology improve and as reading digital texts for facts and fun becomes more common. In the U.S., e-books currently make up more than 20 percent of all books sold to the general public.

Despite all the increasingly user-friendly and popular technology, most studies published since the early 1990s confirm earlier conclusions: paper still has advantages over screens as a reading medium. Together laboratory experiments, polls and consumer reports indicate that digital devices prevent people from efficiently navigating long texts, which may subtly inhibit reading comprehension. Compared with paper, screens may also drain more of our mental resources while we are reading and make it a little harder to remember what we read when we are done. Whether they realize it or not, people often approach computers and tablets with a state of mind less conducive to learning than the one they bring to paper. And e-readers fail to re-create certain tactile experiences of reading on paper, the absence of which some find unsettling.

"There is physicality in reading," says cognitive scientist Maryanne Wolf of Tufts University, "maybe even more than we want to think about as we lurch into digital reading–as we move forward perhaps with too little reflection. I would like to preserve the absolute best of older forms but know when to use the new."

Textual Landscapes

Understanding how reading on paper differs from reading on screens requires some explanation of how the human brain interprets written language. Although letters and words are symbols representing sounds and ideas, the brain also regards them as physical objects. As Wolf explains in her 2007 book *Proust and the Squid*, we are not born with brain circuits dedicated to reading, because we did not invent writing until relatively recently in our evolutionary history, around the fourth millennium b.c. So in childhood, the brain improvises a brand-new circuit for reading by weaving together various ribbons of neural tissue devoted to other abilities, such as speaking, motor coordination and vision.

Some of these repurposed brain regions specialize in object recognition: they help us instantly distinguish an apple from an orange, for example, based on their distinct features, yet classify both as fruit. Similarly, when we learn to read and write, we begin to recognize letters by their particular arrangements of lines, curves and hollow spaces–a tactile learning process that requires both our eyes and hands. In recent research by Karin James of Indiana University Bloomington, the reading circuits of five-year-old children crackled with activity when they practiced writing letters by hand but not when they typed letters on a keyboard. And when people read cursive writing or intricate characters such as Japanese *kanji*, the brain literally goes through the motions of writing, even if the hands are empty.

Beyond treating individual letters as physical objects, the human brain may also perceive a text in its entirety as a kind of physical landscape. When we read, we construct a mental representation of the text. The exact nature of such representations remains unclear, but some researchers think they are similar to the mental maps we create of terrain–such as mountains and trails–and of indoor physical spaces, such as apartments and offices. Both anecdotally and in published studies, people report that when trying to locate a particular passage in a book, they often remember where in the text it appeared. Much as we might recall that we passed the red farmhouse near the start of a hiking trail before we started climbing uphill through the forest, we remember that we read about Mr. Darcy rebuffing Elizabeth Bennett at a dance on the bottom left corner of the left-hand page in one of the earlier chapters of Jane Austen's *Pride and Prejudice*.

In most cases, paper books have more obvious topography than on-screen text. An open paper book presents a reader with two clearly defined domains–the left- and right-hand pages–and a total of eight corners with which to orient oneself. You can focus on a single page of a paper book without losing awareness of the whole text. You can even feel the thickness of the pages you have read in one hand and the pages you have yet to read in the other. Turning the pages of a paper book is like leaving one footprint after another on a trail—there is a rhythm to it and a visible record of how far one has traveled. All these features not only make the text in a paper book easily navigable, they also make it easier to form a coherent mental map of that text.

In contrast, most digital devices interfere with intuitive navigation of a text and inhibit people from mapping the journey in their mind. A reader of digital text might scroll through a seamless stream of words, tap forward one page at a time or use the search function to immediately locate a particular phrase—but it is difficult to see any one passage in the context of the entire text. As an analogy, imagine if Google Maps allowed people to navigate street by individual street, as well as to teleport to any specific address, but prevented them from zooming out to see a neighborhood, state or country. Likewise, glancing at a progress bar gives a far more vague sense of place than feeling the weight of read and unread pages. And although e-readers and tablets replicate pagination, the displayed pages are ephemeral. Once read, those pages vanish. Instead of hiking the trail yourself, you watch the trees, rocks and moss pass by in flashes, with no tangible trace of what came before and no easy way to see what lies ahead.

"The implicit feel of where you are in a physical book turns out to be more important than we realized," says Abigail J. Sellen of Microsoft Research Cambridge in England, who co-authored the 2001 book *The Myth of the Paperless Office*. "Only when you get an e-book do you start to miss it. I don't think e-book manufacturers have thought enough about how you might visualize where you are in a book."

Exhaustive Reading

At least a few studies suggest that screens sometimes impair comprehension precisely because they distort people's sense of place in a text. In a January 2013 study by Anne Mangen of the University of Stavanger in Norway and her colleagues, 72 10th grade students studied one narrative and one expository text. Half the students read on paper, and half read PDF files on computers. Afterward, students completed reading comprehension tests, during which they had access to the texts. Students who read the texts on computers performed a little worse, most likely because they had to scroll or click through the PDFs one section at a time, whereas students reading on paper held the entire texts in their hands and quickly switched between different pages. "The ease with which you can find out the beginning, end, and everything in between and the constant connection to your path, your progress in the text, might be some way of making it less taxing cognitively," Mangen says. "You have more free capacity for comprehension."

Other researchers agree that screen-based reading can dull comprehension because it is more mentally taxing and even physically tiring than reading on paper. E-ink reflects ambient light just like the ink on a paper book, but computer screens, smartphones and tablets shine light directly on people's faces. Today's LCDs are certainly gentler on eyes than their predecessor, cathode-ray tube (CRT) screens, but prolonged reading on glossy, self-illuminated screens can cause eyestrain, headaches and blurred vision. In an experiment by Erik Wästlund, then at Karlstad University in Sweden, people who took a reading comprehension test on a computer scored lower and reported higher levels of stress and tiredness than people who completed it on paper.

In a related set of Wästlund's experiments, 82 volunteers completed the same reading comprehension test on computers, either as a paginated document or as a continuous piece of text. Afterward, researchers assessed the students' attention and working memory–a collection of mental talents allowing people to temporarily store and manipulate information in their mind. Volunteers had to quickly close a series of pop-up windows, for example, or remember digits that flashed on a screen. Like many cognitive abilities, working memory is a finite resource that diminishes with exertion.

Although people in both groups performed equally well, those who had to scroll through the unbroken text did worse on the attention and working memory tests. Wästlund thinks that scrolling–which requires readers to consciously focus on both the text and how they are moving it–drains more mental resources than turning or clicking a page, which are simpler and more automatic gestures. The more attention is diverted to moving through a text, the less is available for understanding it. A 2004 study conducted at the University of Central Florida reached similar conclusions.

An emerging collection of studies emphasizes that in addition to screens possibly leeching more attention than paper, people do not always bring as much mental effort to screens in the first place. Based on a detailed 2005 survey of 113 people in northern California, Ziming Liu of San Jose State University concluded that those reading on screens take a lot of shortcuts–they spend more time browsing, scanning and hunting for keywords compared with people reading on paper and are more likely to read a document once and only once.

When reading on screens, individuals seem less inclined to engage in what psychologists call metacognitive learning regulation–setting specific goals, rereading difficult sections and checking how much one has understood along the way. In a 2011 experiment at the Technion–Israel Institute of Technology, college students took multiple-choice exams about expository texts either on computers or on paper. Researchers limited half the volunteers to a meager seven minutes of study time; the other half could review the text for as long as they liked. When under pressure to read quickly, students using computers and paper performed equally well. When managing their own study time, however, volunteers using paper scored about 10 percentage points higher. Presumably, students using paper approached the exam with a more studious attitude than their screen-reading peers and more effectively directed their attention and working memory.

Even when studies find few differences in reading comprehension between screens and paper, screen readers may not remember a text as thoroughly in the long run. In a 2003 study Kate Garland, then at the University of Leicester in England, and her team asked 50 British college students to read documents from an introductory economics course either on a computer monitor or in a spiral-bound booklet. After 20 minutes of reading, Garland and her colleagues quizzed the students. Participants scored equally well regardless of the medium but differed in how they remembered the information.

Psychologists distinguish between remembering something–a relatively weak form of memory in which someone recalls a piece of information, along with contextual details, such as where and when one learned it–and knowing something: a stronger form of memory defined as certainty that something is true. While taking the quiz, Garland's volunteers marked both their answer and whether they "remembered" or "knew" the answer. Students who had read study material on a screen relied much more on remembering than on knowing, whereas students who read on paper depended equally on the two forms of memory. Garland and her colleagues think that students who read on paper learned the study material more thoroughly more quickly; they did not have to spend a lot of time searching their mind for information from the text–they often just knew the answers.

Perhaps any discrepancies in reading comprehension between paper and screens will shrink as people's attitudes continue to change. Maybe the star of *A Magazine Is an iPad That Does Not Work* will grow up without the subtle bias against screens that seems to lurk among older generations. The latest research suggests, however, that substituting screens for paper at an early age has disadvantages that we should not write off so easily. A 2012 study at the Joan Ganz Cooney Center in New York City recruited 32 pairs of parents and three- to six-year-old children. Kids remembered more details from stories they read on paper than ones they read in e-books enhanced with interactive animations, videos and games. These bells and whistles deflected attention away from the narrative toward the device itself. In a follow-up survey of 1,226 parents, the majority reported that they and their children prefer print books over e-books when reading together.

Nearly identical results followed two studies, described this past September in *Mind, Brain, and Education*, by Julia Parrish-Morris, now at the University of Pennsylvania, and her colleagues. When reading paper books to their three- and five-year-old children, parents helpfully related the story to their child's life. But when reading a then popular electric console book with sound effects, parents frequently had to interrupt their usual "dialogic reading" to stop the child from fiddling with buttons and losing track of the narrative. Such distractions ultimately prevented the three-year-olds from understanding even the gist of the stories, but all the children followed the stories in paper books just fine.

Such preliminary research on early readers underscores a quality of paper that may be its greatest strength as a reading medium: its modesty. Admittedly, digital texts offer clear advantages in many different situations. When one is researching under deadline, the convenience of quickly accessing hundreds of keyword-searchable online documents vastly outweighs the benefits in comprehension and retention that come with dutifully locating and rifling through paper books one at a time in a library. And for people with poor vision, adjustable font size and the sharp contrast of an LCD screen are godsends. Yet paper, unlike screens, rarely calls attention to itself or shifts focus away from the text. Because of its simplicity, paper is "a still point, an anchor for the consciousness," as William Powers writes in his 2006 essay "Hamlet's Blackberry: Why Paper Is Eternal." People consistently report that when they really want to focus on a text, they read it on paper. In a 2011 survey of graduate students at National Taiwan University, the majority reported browsing a few paragraphs of an item online before printing out the whole text for more in-depth reading. And in a 2003 survey at the National Autonomous University of Mexico, nearly 80 percent of 687 students preferred to read text on paper rather than on a screen to "understand it with clarity."

Beyond pragmatic considerations, the way we feel about a paper book or an e-reader–and the way it feels in our hands–also determines whether we buy a best-selling book in hardcover at a local bookstore or download it from Amazon. Surveys and consumer reports suggest that the sensory aspects of reading on paper matter to people more than one might assume: the feel of paper and ink; the option to smooth or fold a page with one's fingers; the distinctive sound a page makes when turned. So far digital texts have not satisfyingly replicated such sensations. Paper books also have an immediately discernible size, shape and weight. We might refer to a hardcover edition of Leo Tolstoy's *War and Peace* as a "hefty tome" or to a paperback of Joseph Conrad's *Heart of Darkness* as a "slim volume." In contrast, although a digital text has a length that may be represented with a scroll or progress bar, it has no obvious shape or thickness. An e-reader always weighs the same, regardless of whether you are reading Marcel Proust's magnum opus or one of Ernest Hemingway's short stories. Some researchers have found that these discrepancies create enough so-called haptic dissonance to dissuade some people from using e-readers.

To amend this sensory incongruity, many designers have worked hard to make the e-reader or tablet experience as close to reading on paper as possible. E-ink resembles typical chemical ink, and the simple layout of the Kindle's screen looks remarkably like a page in a paper book. Likewise, Apple's iBooks app attempts to simulate somewhat realistic page turning. So far such gestures have been more aesthetic than pragmatic. E-books still prevent people from quickly scanning ahead on a whim or easily flipping to a previous chapter when a sentence surfaces a memory of something they read earlier.

Some digital innovators are not confining themselves to imitations of paper books. Instead they are evolving screen-based reading into something else entirely. Scrolling may not be the ideal way to navigate a text as long and dense as Herman Melville's *Moby Dick*, but the *New York Times*, the *Washington Post*, ESPN and other media outlets have created beautiful, highly visual articles that could not appear in print because they blend text with movies and embedded sound clips and depend entirely on scrolling to create a cinematic experience. Robin Sloan has pioneered the tap essay, which relies on physical interaction to set the pace and tone, unveiling new words, sentences and images only when someone taps a phone or a tablet's touch screen. And some writers are pairing up with computer programmers to produce ever more sophisticated interactive fiction and nonfiction in which one's choices determine what one reads, hears and sees next.

When it comes to intensively reading long pieces of unembellished text, paper and ink may still have the advantage. But plain text is not the only way to read.

About the Author

Ferris Jabr is an associate editor at Scientific American.

Section 2: Virtually Socialized

Want to Ease the Isolation of Social Distancing? Ask a Teenager

By Alexandra O. Cohen

"Stay home."

This suddenly universal call to maintain physical distance from other people, known as social distancing, is key to combating the spread of the coronavirus, according to health professionals. Yet the potential for unprecedented loneliness as people isolate themselves has spurred calls for maintaining social connections. As we shift our vocational and educational endeavors into the online world, we must also go virtual with many of our relationships to sustain our social lives.

One group knows how to do this better than any other: teens.

Changes in the importance and complexity of our social world largely define the teenage years. The current generation is growing up with cell phones, social media and an increasing number of ways to connect through technology. As a consequence, they are notorious for their affinity for screens. Teens' use of technology tends to evoke negative sentiments, occasionally including the doom and destruction of a generation, despite the lack of conclusive data supporting this narrative. But now, as the coronavirus crisis infiltrates our daily lives, we all find ourselves turning to technology to maintain social connections. Who better to teach us than the people who know how to use it?

Although public perception is that screens are damaging this generation, most teenagers would actually tell you that technology helps them build positive relationships. A 2018 Pew Research Center report shows that 81 percent of teens believe that social media helps them feel more connected to their friends. Despite acknowledging some drawbacks, they report that social media supports their friendships and allows them to engage with individuals from various backgrounds, with differing viewpoints.

Teens use a variety of technological means beyond just social media to keep in constant communication with their friends. Other modes of connection include text messaging, instant messaging, messaging on apps, phone calls, video chats, video gaming, and the list (believe it or not) goes on. In fact, 57 percent of teens have made new friends online. Meanwhile, the average American adult hasn't made a new friend in five years. If maintaining meaningful human connection is what we are after, these data suggest that teens, more than adults, have the expertise to make that happen.

As we face a health crisis that alters the way we conduct our daily lives, teens might have solutions to some of the new problems we're encountering. Today's young people have already emerged as leaders, championing stances on major issues affecting us all such as climate change and gun control. High schoolers are now demonstrating the ability to adapt to the current conditions by planning virtual proms and looking ahead towards plans for graduation.

Parents have an opportunity to empower their kids and themselves as social distancing forces families to spend more time together under one roof. Rather than fear unknown future consequences of technology use, parents can start a dialogue with their children about how they use technology right now. Parents can encourage teens to teach the art of virtual camaraderie to them, aunts, uncles, grandparents, and others who could benefit from increased interaction while physically isolated. Giving young people the opportunity to teach may have added benefits of helping teens build their confidence, communication skills and cross-generational connections (beyond merely serving as tech support).

Let's talk to young people. Let's embrace the virtual communication skills they have cultivated and ask them to show the rest of us how they use technology to stay connected. Let's give them the opportunity to help keep us close during social distancing.

The views expressed are those of the author(s) and are not necessarily those of Scientific American.

About the Author

Alexandra O. Cohen, Ph.D., is a postdoctoral fellow in developmental cognitive neuroscience at NYU who focuses on how motivation shapes learning and memory across adolescence.

The Death of Social Reciprocity in the Era of Digital Distraction

By Brian Solis

You're walking along the street, and bump into a friend. After a quick hello, this friend compliments you. What do you do in response? Most likely, offer a compliment in return. Or, at the least, say thank you.

A few steps further down the street, you see someone drop a wallet. You pick it up and hand it to them. They say thank you. Your response: "You're welcome."

For most of us, interactions throughout each day are filled with social reciprocity. It's instantaneous and second nature. Even chimps have been shown to engage in it. It can be a very good thing. But in recent years, digital distraction has turned it into a problem.

As I explain in my book *Lifescale*, many creators of digital platforms have studied psychology. Their goal has been to eat up more and more of our days. Through persuasive design, they've worked to manipulate human behavior.

After all, the attention economy is wildly lucrative. Our attention is the currency; it's what we pay to use these platforms for free. It's also finite, so there's limited supply and great demand. Netflix CEO Reed Hastings once said his company's number one competitor was sleep. "And, we're winning!"

Having spent years in Silicon Valley as a digital futurist and adviser to many social media companies, I've seen the myriad ways the purveyors of these technologies work to get users addicted. They've been so successful that there's even a term for fear of being without your cell phone, "nomophobia." One trick that gets too little attention (pun intended) is the psychological hijack of social reciprocity.

In the digital world, interactions take place at an unprecedented pace. People like or share your posts and tag you in theirs. They send you connection requests or follow you, and often expect you to do the same in return. Notifications show people when you have read their messages, so they might find it rude if you don't respond relatively soon. After you respond, you see those wavering dots of someone composing a reply to you, so you know the conversation is continuing.

All of this makes you feel anticipation and pressure to stay engaged, respond, check back and interact. *Vice* reported in 2017 that Snapchat's elongating red lines displaying "the number of days since two users interacted" even reportedly led some teens to ask friends "to babysit their streaks"–that is, to interact on their behalf–while they were on vacation.

This is the new norm. We've been fooled into believing we're more connected, informed, productive, creative and happy. But in reality, this kind of social reciprocity eats away at our norms and values, and rebuilds them in harmful ways. As a former Facebook executive put it, "The short-term, dopamine-driven feedback loops that we have created are destroying how society works."

I know from experience what a toll this can take. Several years ago, I found myself struggling. I couldn't concentrate on work, and often wasn't fully present with my family.

I was totally distracted, being drawn to notification after notification. I'd tell myself not to reach for my phone. But within minutes (or seconds), I'd nevertheless be checking out a picture that a friend just posted on Instagram, and composing a response to let him know that I'd seen and enjoyed it.

A year went by before I realized I had to press pause on all of it. I wasn't just losing productivity, but also my creative spark and even my ability to feel happiness. Worst of all, my relationships were suffering.

To tackle the part of your mind that feels–instinctively–that you owe it to people to reciprocate, I recommend two key steps:

1. Honor Your Right to Disconnect

In 2017, France officially gave workers the "right to disconnect" from e-mail after work hours.

What if we take that idea and broaden it out? We all have a right to disconnect from the bombardment of notifications. And that means we have a right to not reciprocate instantly to online interactions.

Thinking of it this way, as a right, can be psychologically empowering.

2. Focus on Strengthening Real Relationships

The other step is to focus on strengthening your relationships with those closest to you by carving out time for them.

In *Lifescale*, I explain the steps I took to overcome my tech addiction. One was to list the values most important to me and the actions I would take to honor them. As part of this, I vowed in writing to carve out uninterrupted time for family and help those relationships grow and thrive.

By keeping in mind that interaction online took time away from work or family, I learned to ease off the pressure of digital social reciprocity. I took back control.

So, yes, some people don't hear back from me as quickly as they used to. I hear all the time from people who are genuinely upset with me about that. But my personal life and career have never been better.

The views expressed are those of the author(s) and are not necessarily those of Scientific American.

About the Author

Brian Solis is principal analyst and futurist at BrianSolis.com and the author of Lifescale: How to Live a More Creative, Productive, and Happy Life.

The Technology of Kindness

By Jamil Zaki

In the run-up to the 1964 World's Fair, the great science-fiction writer Isaac Asimov was asked what that same event might look like 50 years later. He guessed that by 2014, we'd be in the constant company of "electroluminescent panels"–used for video chat, navigation and, more deeply, "to withdraw from nature in order to create an environment that will suit [us] better."

Asimov's future is our present. This worries many people, who think technology has left us dumber, sadder and meaner than we were before. Empathy–people's ability to share and understand one another's emotions–has declined sharply in the 21st century. If it dies out, technology will probably be charged with the murder. The clues are all there: People in countries with a greater Internet penetrance report lower empathy. Simply leaving a phone between two strangers as they talk lessens their resulting trust. The prosecution's case writes itself: while apparently serving us, technology quietly poisoned the connections that keep us human.

Yet technology, and the Internet in particular, are not inherently antisocial. They can sap our empathy, but used differently, they could become a world-sized magnifying glass for our better angels. Many corners of the Internet already allow people to broaden their empathy and share collective goodwill. Researchers are pinpointing the ingredients of positive technology. If they become the norm, the future of life online will be kinder than its past. Internet platforms must heed this evidence, and their users must demand them to do so.

People's ability to connect is the glue that holds our culture together. By thinning out our interactions and splintering our media landscape, the Internet has taken away the common ground we need to understand one another. Each of us is becoming more confident about our own world just as it drifts farther from the worlds of others. Empathy requires us to understand that even people who disagree with us have a lived experience as deep as our own. But in the fractured landscape of social media, we have little choice but to see the other side as obtuse, dishonest or both. Unless we reverse this trend and revive empathy, we have little chance of mending the tears in our social fabric.

Technology's socially depleting effects are not coincidental; they reflect how platforms such as Facebook and Twitter are designed–and such platforms are, in turn, shaped by financial incentives. These sites satisfy shareholders not by making users healthy or happy but by keeping them online. This imperative favors extremism, vanity, fear–whatever grabs us and holds on. About 70 percent of YouTube views now come from the site's recommendations, which are optimized to generate clicks. The result is a massive flow of eyeballs to conspiracy theories, bigotry, and aggression. This is what former Google ethicist Tristan Harris calls "extractive" technology: it takes advantage of our frailties and gets more effective at harming us as it grows more sophisticated.

Life online changes how we see others and how we are seen. Sometimes we're not seen at all–our face and name is replaced by an avatar and an anonymous character string. Anonymity can be vital–for instance, by allowing people to safely organize protests in totalitarian nations. But it also cuts the brake lines on social interactions, encouraging people to try cruelty on like a mask, knowing it won't cost them. Cyberbullying follows people into their homes and beds and leaves its victims more suicidal than those of traditional bullying.

When we are seen online, the Internet's token economy can pervert how we present ourselves. In a 2017 study, psychologist William Brady and his colleagues analyzed more than 500,000 tweets to examine what makes them go viral. They found that the more "moral emotion"–such as outrage–a post contained, the more it was retweeted, especially within the original poster's ideological circles. Retweets are tiny, addictive affirmations, which reinforce outrage. After being rewarded with attention, people responded by making their later tweets even more aggrieved than before. Twitter not only reflects an angry world; it helps create one.

Social media makes us less social when it replaces rich, analog hangouts with strings of text and curated images. In a 2017 set of studies, Juliana Schroeder of the University of California, Berkeley, and her colleagues taped individuals as they described their opinion on polarizing political issues. A separate set of "evaluators" either listened to those recordings or read their transcripts. Evaluators were more likely to dehumanize speakers when their opinions were reduced to text, especially when the evaluators disagreed with them. Thinned-out interactions made empathy harder to access.

Diagnosing technology's damaging effects is the first step toward reversing them. Harris co-founded the Center for Humane Technology to encourage developers and investors to build "regenerative," rather than extractive, online platforms. The idea is that our capacity for empathy runs just as deep as our vanity, outrage or fear, and technology should highlight healthier forces.

Some sites are purposefully built to favor connection and understanding. On ChangeAView, people post their opinion on a range of topics, inviting fellow posters to persuade them otherwise. Commenters are rewarded not for trolling or shaming but for "deltas"—an indication their argument changed someone's mind. The result is a feast of thoughtful, genuine dialogue among people who might not otherwise engage with one another.

Technology also builds new communities around kindness. Consider the paradox of rare illnesses such as cystic fibrosis or myasthenia gravis. Each affects fewer than one in 1,000 people, but there are many such conditions, meaning there are many people who suffer in ways their friends and neighbors don't understand. Millions have turned to online forums, such as Facebook groups or the site RareConnect. In 2011 Priya Nambisan, a health policy expert, surveyed about 800 members of online health forums. Users reported that these groups offer helpful tips and information but also described them as heartfelt communities, full of compassion and commiseration.

Other platforms, such as Koko and 7 Cups, have scaled this approach, allowing anyone to count on the kindness of strangers.

These sites train users to provide empathetic social support and then unleash their goodwill on one another. Some express their struggles; others step in to provide support. Users find these platforms deeply soothing. In a 2015 survey, 7 Cups users described the kindness they received on the site to be as helpful as professional psychotherapy. Users on these sites also benefit from helping others. In a 2017 study, psychologist Bruce Doré and his colleagues assigned people to use either Koko or another Web site and tested their subsequent well-being. Koko users' levels of depression dropped after spending time on the site, especially when they used it to support others.

Sites such as ChangeAView and 7 Cups can appear like oases of connection in a landscape bereft of it—exceptions that prove the rule. But what sets connected platforms apart is their break from common, antisocial online practices. They allow people to be vulnerable and visible to one another and reward them for listening rather than shouting. Other social media companies could follow suit: by reforming their incentive structures such that open-minded, positive posts rise more quickly or by facilitating longer, richer communication between users. But they must make progress on this mission intentionally and soon.

Mark Zuckerberg famously exhorted his employees to "move fast and break things." By now, it's clear they've broken quite a lot. No matter how much we decry the effects of technology, there's no going back. But we can get better at detecting what life online does to us and how it could do better. This could begin with the companies that build social media platforms, but users could be forgiven for not trusting tech giants to have our best interests in mind. Restorative online technology will grow only when we demand it from them.

About the Author

Jamil Zaki is an associate professor of psychology at Stanford University and director of the Stanford Social Neuroscience Laboratory. He is author of The War for Kindness.

For a Better Connection, Talk Instead of Typing

By Amit Kumar

Throughout the COVID-19 pandemic, the term "social distancing" has been at the center of public conversation, but this phrase is a bit of a misnomer. Taken literally, the phrase seems to endorse social separation. But it's not "social" distance we are trying to promote. It's physical separation. In fact, preserving social ties—even at a distance—is essential for both mental and physical health. The results of epidemiological meta-analyses, for example, indicate that a lack of social support is on par with smoking cigarettes as a risk factor for morbidity and mortality and is even more harmful than other stressors, such as obesity and air pollution. Given this empirical fact, how might we best stay connected to others while maintaining physical distance? Would we better off e-mailing a friend? Making a phone call? Setting up a video chat? Modern technology has provided us with many tools at our disposal. Not all tools foster social connection equally, however. And often such seemingly small choices can make a big difference between cultivating stronger social connections and giving in to growing social distance.

In a paper soon to be published in the *Journal of Experimental Psychology: General*, Nick Epley and I tested whether the media through which people interact affects their sense of connection—and how expectations about certain technologies impact the communication media they choose to use. Note that these expectations can be misguided. Although voice-based interactions (such as phone calls) can produce stronger connections, text-based media (such as e-mails) are often preferred because of mistaken beliefs about how social interactions will unfold. Any interaction we have can come with advantages and disadvantages, and decisions about how to connect tend to be based on expectations of these potential costs and benefits. When people overestimate the cost, or underestimate the benefit, of voice-based communication, it can create a misplaced bias for text-based media.

In one experiment, for instance, we asked participants to reconnect with someone that they hadn't interacted with recently, either through e-mail or over the phone. Participants first made predictions about what it would be like to get in touch if they reached out in these two ways. More specifically, these participants predicted how connected and how awkward they would feel in each situation. In this experiment, they did generally intuit that they'd feel more connected when interacting via the phone than over e-mail. But they also predicted that talking on the phone could be more uncomfortable than dashing off an e-mail. Participants additionally indicated which option they preferred. Although these participants believed that talking encouraged stronger bonds, most of them said they'd rather send an e-mail than call the person up. Fears about awkwardness, it seems, push individuals toward text-based methods for communicating.

Our results demonstrated that, contrary to participants' expectations, worries about awkwardness are largely unwarranted. In the next part of the experiment, we had participants actually reconnect using one randomly determined mode of communication—either e-mail or phone—and then followed up with them after they had done so. As expected, we found that people do form meaningfully stronger bonds when interacting over the phone than over e-mail. Importantly, though, there was no difference in the amount of discomfort when reconnecting on the phone. The human voice appears to provide benefits for connection without the expected costs.

In another experiment, we had individuals connect with each other by asking and answering a series of relatively personal questions (for example, "Is there something you've dreamed of doing for a long time? Why haven't you done it?"). These conversations took place by texting in real time during a live chat, using only audio, or engaging in a video chat. Once again, participants first made predictions about how they believed they would feel and then actually had a discussion with someone else. We again measured awkwardness and connection, in this case using statements such as how much they would get to know their conversation partner, how much they would like that person, and how strong of a bond they would feel. Here, participants didn't expect that the media through which they communicated would matter. But when they actually interacted, people again felt significantly more connected–and notably, no more awkward–when they communicated by talking rather than typing. Interestingly, visual cues didn't add more to what voice-based media already provided. Media containing only audio, as in a phone call, created as strong a sense of connection as audiovisual media, and both produced higher-quality social interactions than text-based media.

Our work suggests that these miscalibrated expectations can affect how people choose to connect with others and therefore how well they do so. Misunderstanding the costs and benefits of different interactions can lead individuals to choose inferior methods for connecting, leading them to text, e-mail, or send a message on Slack instead of picking up the phone, which results in a more positive interaction. In light of this evidence, it is critical that we not only focus on the content we are trying to convey but also the context in which it is conveyed. The next time you think about how best to connect, consider calling or setting up a video chat. You're likely to feel better as a result. E-mail or text messaging can sometimes be useful for sending attachments or scheduling a time to talk, to be sure. Feelings of social connection, however, are optimally facilitated by one's voice rather than their keyboard.

About the Author

Amit Kumar is an assistant professor of marketing and psychology at the University of Texas at Austin. He received his A.B. in psychology and economics from Harvard University and his Ph.D. in social psychology from Cornell University.

The Benefits of Being Yourself Online

By Erica R. Bailey and Sandra Matz

With a steady stream of avocado toast, latte art and vintage Huji filters, Instagram advertises the kind of life to which almost anyone would aspire. If you take social media's word for it, the world is full of happy, healthy, thriving people taking luxury vacations, getting drinks with lifelong friends and promoting their passion projects online. Even amid a global pandemic and record levels of social isolation, many still fall prey to the glossy perfection of the feed.

But celebrities such as Chrissy Teigen and Dax Shepard have gone in a different direction, inspiring millions of users by sharing both the mundane and raw experiences of real life. Are people happier and more satisfied when they present themselves in a way that feels real or when they share a self-idealized version of their life? In our research, published in *Nature Communications*, we set out to tackle this question and determine how individuals' online image actually affects them.

Our starting point was a data set of more than 10,000 Facebook users who had completed a personality questionnaire and volunteered to have their Facebook profile information used for scientific purposes. This unique data set allowed us to compare the way that people see themselves (i.e., their responses to the personality questions) with how they portray themselves to their social network and the world through their posts and the pages they follow (i.e., computer-based predictions of their personality from Facebook posts and pages).

For example, "Jane" might think of herself as an introvert and describe herself as such in a questionnaire. If she posted on social media in the way introverts typically do (e.g., talking about reading, books or computers), her social media authenticity score would be high. In other words, her self-view would match the way she expressed herself to others. In contrast, if Jane were to describe herself as an introvert but post in a way that is typical of extraverts (e.g., talking about parties or weekends out), her social media authenticity score would be low.

Mapping this authenticity score to participants' level of life satisfaction (i.e., the extent to which they evaluated the overall conditions of their life as positive and desirable) showed that those who expressed themselves in a more authentic–rather than self-idealized–way reported more satisfaction with their life. A clear win for Teigen and Shepard!

Yet one of the questions that came up was: "Is this really true for everybody? Sure, if I am an emotionally stable extravert, posting authentically might be great. It's who I am but also who everybody else wants me to be. What if I am neurotic and an introvert instead? Would I benefit equally from being my authentic self?" So we went back to our data to test that. As it turns out, this worry was largely unfounded. The extent to which authentic self-expression on social media was related to participants' life satisfaction did not depend on how socially desirable their personality profiles were. In other words, both extraverts and introverts benefitted equally from being true to themselves.

But does authentic expression actually lead to higher levels of life satisfaction? Or is it the case that people who are more satisfied with their lives find it easier to post authentically? To show that posting in an authentic way was indeed driving well-being, we followed up on our initial study with an experiment to demonstrate causality.

For this experiment, we recruited social media users and randomly assigned them to either post in a way that was authentic (based on their personality) or post in a way that was popular and made them look good in the eyes of others. After a week spent following these instructions, we switched the groups: the people who had initially posted in an authentic way were then asked to post in an idealized way, and vice versa. Supporting our initial finding, we discovered that after posting in an authentic way for a week, participants reported higher levels of positive affect and mood than they did after the week in which they posted to please others.

Our findings can't speak to the question of whether using social media is better than not using it at all. Abstaining from social media altogether might yield the highest levels of life satisfaction. But our results do suggest that if you use social media regularly, you should try not to fall prey to the perfection–instead just be yourself!

About the Authors

Erica R. Bailey is a Ph.D. candidate at Columbia Business School. She studies authenticity, examining both what makes people feel like themselves and what makes them seem authentic to others.

Sandra Matz is the David W. Zalaznick Associate Professor of Business at Columbia Business School. As a computational social scientist, she studies human behavior and preferences using a combination of big data analytics and traditional experimental methods.

Stretched Too Thin by Social Media

By Brett Frischmann

In the past two months, I received multiple invitations to leave Facebook and Twitter and join a new social network that promises to not destroy democracy. I'm tempted. I'm also tempted to delete my accounts and abandon social media altogether. The decision got me thinking, not about democracy but instead about how social media affect my behavior and relationships.

Social media promise and deliver social networks with better or at least bigger scale and scope. Essentially, this means you can connect to many more people from many different places to relate on a wider variety of interests. To socialize is a core human need. The difficult question is whether social media improve our capability to relate to each other.

The answer may seem obvious. Social media afford connectivity, engagement and relationship management at such incredible scale and in such a convenient manner. It must be a substantial improvement. Most social media users can attest to the power. Many will recall that thrill of finding lost friends, connecting with distant colleagues, or maintaining relationships that would otherwise be forgotten or just lost.

Yet, paradoxically, the feeling of power may, like the rush from an intoxicant, blind users to deleterious consequences. Social media can be vampiric on human attention, empathy and care. Consider the ad-based business model upon which most social media depend. Attention is bought and sold. Social media serve as the gateway to behavioral data extraction while delivering targeted stimuli–whether ads or inducements to keep you glued to the platform.

We only have so much time, energy and attention to devote to our relationships, to make them meaningful.

Social media change how we relate to each other. But are we better or worse off? To evaluate that question, we need baselines.

Without social media, people have many different social networks, from intimate to professional. Consider the most intimate social network, your family. Families are social networks where, in network lingo, family members are the "nodes," and the "ties" (sometimes called "links") between nodes may be stronger/weaker based on the relationship between nodes. Thus, parent-child and sibling ties are much stronger than distant cousin ties.

When my wife and I got engaged, we would tell folks that we planned to have a large family. I grew up with seven siblings, and that gave me a benchmark. My wife had two siblings and many close cousins, and she worked with children. We figured we would have six or more children!

We now have three boys and do not plan on having any more. After transitioning from man-to-man to zone defense, we realized that three was more than enough. We could only afford that many. And not just financially. Honestly, if we had infinite financial, emotional and other resources and we ignored broader environmental considerations, we would love to have more children. But scarcity is a fact of life, despite what some abundance evangelists preach.

My wife and I realized that with three children, our attention was spread as far as we thought was appropriate for us to be meaningfully engaged in our children's and our own lives. Our immediate family of five sustains strong ties. We worried that expanding our network would risk weakening them. Of course, we never used those words! We would say we didn't want to stretch ourselves too thin.

Lately, this is how I feel when I use social media platforms–stretched too thin, maintaining relationships with large numbers of weak ties, often though not always with superficial forms of engagement. Worse, I find myself devoting time, attention and effort to people with whom I have no actual tie at all. Even weaker than weak ties are the nonexisting relationships, the potential ties many of us find ourselves catering to on social media platforms. Potential followers, a potential audience, people who follow people who follow me who just might receive a shared post or tweet. It sounds ridiculous when actually written, doesn't it? Yet if you use social media platforms, you probably know what I'm talking about.

What's so bad about being stretched thin? Well, there are trade-offs, which vary for different people. In general, I'm concerned with the impact on strong ties, our most important and meaningful relationships. Being stretched too thin may weaken strong ties, lead to fewer strong ties, or both. This is the most obvious effect to look out for, but there are other relationships that might be impacted. Consider, for example, your moderate ties, say your co-workers or neighbors. These important relationships might be sacrificed at the social media altar as people seek affirmation and attention from much weaker, less meaningful, but more plentiful ties.

Some might say I'm old-fashioned for putting driveway and watercooler conversations on a pedestal and for denigrating emoji- and click-fueled communications. That's not really the point though. I struggle with social media too. Evaluating the trade-offs isn't easy. But an important first step is recognizing that it's about more than democracy writ large, the algorithms structuring what you encounter, or the specific content in your feed. It is fundamentally about the nature and strength of the relationships you cultivate.

The views expressed are those of the author(s) and are not necessarily those of Scientific American.

About the Author

Brett Frischmann is the Charles Widger Endowed University Professor in Law, Business and Economics at Villanova University. His latest nonfiction book is Re-Engineering Humanity *(Cambridge University Press, 2018). His novel is* Shephard's Drone *(independently published, 2019)*.

How to Silence Cyberbullying

By Elizabeth Svoboda

When 25-year-old Caitlin Seida dressed up as Lara Croft from the movie *Tomb Raider* one Halloween, she posted a picture of herself enjoying the night's festivities on Facebook. At most, she figured a few friends might see the photograph and comment.

The picture remained in Seida's social circle for more than three years. Then one day in 2013 a friend sent Seida a link with a cryptic note: "You're Internet famous." Clicking the link took her to a site called the International Association of Haters, where her Halloween photo—which she had posted publicly by mistake—bore the oversized caption "Fridge Raider." Hundreds of commenters dragged Seida through the mud for wearing a skimpy costume while being overweight. "Heifers like her should be put down," one commenter wrote. "What a waste of space," another piped in.

Horrified, Seida did some more quick searches and realized her photo had gone viral, racking up poisonous comments on dozens of sites. Reading the messages was like absorbing a series of body blows. "I felt like shit," Seida says. "I cried and cried and cried some more." With a paralegal friend's help, she contacted Web site owners to get the offending images and posts taken down, but she knew her efforts would likely fall short. "I can herd cats more easily than I can control what's posted online."

Despite the publicity devoted to teenage cyberbullies, online aggression is hardly confined to the high school set. About one in four adults has been cyberbullied or knows someone who has, according to a recent poll by the online design firm Rad Campaign, along with Lincoln Park Strategies and Craigslist founder Craig Newmark. The abuse can come in the form of insulting e-mails, tag team–style pile-ons in Internet forums or personal attacks in news article comment sections. Victims are often so profoundly affected that they descend into depression or even contemplate suicide. Yet the problem has largely gone unaddressed because so few observers take it seriously and because it can be unclear which comments qualify as bullying. "People are reluctant to report it," says Chris Piotrowski, a cyberbullying expert and research consultant at the University of West Florida. "A lot of them feel like, '[If] I go to the police, what are they going to do?'"

Researchers are uncovering the psychological forces behind such poisonous verbiage and the harm it causes, and their work points to ways of preventing vicious avalanches of verbal aggression—or at least minimizing the damage. An important part of the solution involves all of us. As members of the Internet democracy, we each have the power to redirect negative group tendencies in ways that promote online civility. "Don't wait for the other two or 300 [people] to do something," says Mary Aiken, director of the CyberPsychology Research Center at the Royal College of Surgeons in Ireland. "It's up to users to create a better environment."

"They Got the Better of Me, and They Won"

The trope of the swaggering bully is almost as old as human history. Whether children or adults, bullies blast their targets with scathing words and profane put-downs—and they do not let up, even when the victim begs for mercy. Bullying behavior probably has evolutionary roots, argues social anthropologist Christopher Boehm of the University of Southern California. Early humans who were good at lording it over others enjoyed a boost in their social standing, and as a result, they produced more offspring.

Contrary to popular wisdom, bullies are not merely compensating for their own low self-esteem. In a 2013 study of thousands of middle school students, psychologist Jaana Juvonen of the University of California, Los Angeles, and her colleagues found that bullies are often perched at the top of the social hierarchy and demean others to cement their position. Upbringing also plays a key role: according to social learning theory, we learn how to interact with others by observing those close to us. Aggressive parents and other role models, then, may produce aggressive kids. The fallout can be devastating: bullying victims suffer significant distress, sometimes for decades. The U.S. Secret Service reports that in most school shooting incidents, shooters felt persecuted or bullied before launching their attacks.

Now that people are socializing in virtual realms, an age-old dynamic has taken hold in a new environment. Cyberbullying is usually defined as intimidation, hurt or harassment conducted using cell phones, the Internet or other electronic devices, but as Piotrowski points out, the contours of this definition are somewhat blurry. "What defines cyberabuse? To one person, it's someone who's being rude. To another person, it's an offensive statement. Another person might say it's [an attack that's] escalating."

At its most obvious, cyberbullying is extremely brutal. Women's-rights activist Caroline Criado-Perez endured dozens of unhinged online trolling attacks from woman haters after she convinced the Bank of England to feature Jane Austen on its 10-pound note. "I remember the man who told me a group of them would mutilate my genitals with scissors and set my house on fire while I begged to die," Criado-Perez told the *New Statesman* in January. "I remember the fear, the horror, the despair. I remember not being able to sleep. I remember thinking it would never end." (Although Criado-Perez did contact the police, she felt they did not take her complaints seriously.)

As Criado-Perez's experience suggests, online persecution can take an outsize toll on mental health. Victims of cyberabuse often show symptoms consistent with post-traumatic stress disorder, including flashbacks, runaway anxiety, guilt or depression. They report low self-esteem and feelings of helplessness. "It's a serious problem that has serious psychological consequences," says social psychologist S. Alexander Haslam of the University of Queensland in Australia. Even people used to the public eye may reach a breaking point when tormentors go too far. Australian journalist Charlotte Dawson–herself an antibullying activist–broke down earlier this year after absorbing a relentless barrage of Twitter messages mocking her depression and encouraging her to kill herself. She was found dead in her Sydney apartment, where she had hanged herself. "It just triggered that feeling of helplessness when the trolls got to me," Dawson said in a 2012 interview on Australia's *60 Minutes* after a previous round of Twitter attacks. "They got the better of me, and they won."

Mob Mentality

Just like real-world bullies, the worst online gangsters often display antisocial personality traits. Some may show characteristics of psychopathy such as aggression and disregard for fellow human beings; others are sadistic. In a 2014 study psychologist Erin E. Buckels of the University of Manitoba and her colleagues surveyed more than 1,200 Internet users and found that those who agreed with statements such as "I enjoy making jokes at the expense of others" and "I enjoy playing the villain in games and torturing other characters" were more likely to show traits associated with personality disorders. It stands to reason that people who have real-life antisocial tendencies might show similar contempt for others in the online realm.

Still, plenty of psychologically balanced adults take online potshots at others, says psychologist John Suler of Rider University, partially because cyberspace lets them create a virtual persona that is separate from their everyday identity. They know that when they retreat behind the cloak of anonymity, they probably will not have to answer for their actions. The phenomenon of the faceless, nameless online bully is a familiar one; surveys suggest only about one in four online bullying victims know their attackers in real life. "From the abuser's point of view, [online bullying] is low risk, high reward," Piotrowski says. "They're thinking, 'I won't get caught because it's online,'" and they get the buzz of feeling elevated because they are pushing someone else down. In a 2012 study psychologists Noam Lapidot-Lefler, now at the Max Stern Academic College of Emek Yezreel, and Azy Barak of the University of Haifa instructed participants to debate a contentious topic in pairs over online chat; they noted that people were more likely to threaten their debate partners when posting under an alias than when using their real names.

But the most noxious and prevalent instances of online bullying emerge from a combination of anonymity and group forces. In 2001 social psychologist Tom Postmes, now at the University of Groningen in the Netherlands, and his colleagues reported that when online participants were anonymous, they were more likely to conform to the behavior of the groups they belonged to–a tendency that is problematic when the group's members are rude or aggressive. Similarly, in a 2012 study psychology researcher Adam Zimmerman of the University of North Florida studied 126 online participants in a word-unscrambling game and found that those who did not use their real names were more likely than identified participants to write aggressive blog posts about their fellow players, especially when they observed other participants acting aggressively. "We get permission [to bully] from the people around us," Zimmerman says. "It gives us the idea that we could also do that if we want to."

When nameless, faceless online participants assume the identity of the group that surrounds them, a virtual mob mentality takes hold. People are impulsive and aggressive and tend to copy one another, often leading to tag-team attacks like those hurled at Seida. "When people engage in online bullying, they are often doing it in front of a particular audience they imagine is approving," Haslam says. If a chat forum's terms of engagement–stated or unstated–allow people to be bullied without consequence, new participants are probably going to conform to the norms set by the bullies. Even people with good intentions can succumb. "If others are piling on someone, you might join in even if you weren't setting out to hurt anyone," adds psychologist Scott O. Lilienfeld of Emory University.

Once insult-slinging gets under way in a chat room or e-mail thread, it can escalate quickly, perhaps because empathy is more elusive in a virtual environment. Cyberaggressors cannot see their victims' tears or the fear in their eyes. Their targets are abstractions. In addition, the bullying persists in ways that would have been unthinkable in the era before Google and Facebook. Victims relive that punch-in-the-gut feeling every time humiliating photos of them appear on a new Web site or insults appear in search results for their name. Also, as Seida learned, erasing the attacks or even getting bullies to admit to the harm they have caused is fiendishly difficult. When Seida and a friend tracked down some of her tormentors and sent them personal notes, they were rebuffed. "We sent them messages and a little certificate that said, 'Why don't you be a human being and take down the comments you made?' Nobody apologized."

Bullying can affect bystanders, too. In a study published in 2013 Colorado State University communications specialist Ashley Anderson and her colleagues recruited more than 1,000 people to read an online article about the risks and benefits of nanotechnology. Readers who were exposed to "flame wars" in which commenters slammed nanotech or insulted its defenders tended to see nanotechnology's risks as more pronounced than did readers who had not seen such verbal attacks, regardless of whether the arguments held water. If, as these results suggest, bullies' comments are often persuasive, passive observers might start to buy into some of the attackers' claims ("Theresa is a slutbag ho").

Setting New Norms

The toxic fallout from online attacks has led some respected news outlets to kill off virtual discussion communities. "We are as committed to fostering lively, intellectual debate as we are to spreading the word of science far and wide," wrote *Popular Science*'s then digital editor Suzanne LaBarre last fall, announcing that the magazine planned to eliminate its Web site's comment section. "The problem is when trolls overwhelm the former, diminishing our ability to do the latter."

The decision by *Popular Science* to nix online comments provoked outcry. Efforts to curb online bullying and flame wars often err in the direction of limiting open discussion. Part of the reason is practical. Policing individual online interactions–by, say, enforcing language restrictions on discussion boards or cleaning up news comment sections–can be a time-consuming task for Web site managers. What is more, few victims report bullying to site administrators because they think nothing will be done about the problem or because they fear retribution from attackers.

So far legislative solutions to the online aggression problem do not seem all that effective, even though 48 states have laws against electronic harassment. California's legal code, for instance, gives administrators grounds to suspend or expel students for participating in online bullying, and Louisiana's legal code reads, "Whoever commits the crime of cyberbullying shall be fined not more than five hundred dollars, imprisoned for not more than six months, or both." Such laws, however, are seldom enforced, in part because cyberbullying victims do not always report being abused—and when victims do complain, administrators and discussion board owners do not always notify state authorities.

In the absence of systematic policing by Web site managers or the government, some administrators have begun testing automated antibullying tools. A system produced by the video game company Riot Games, for instance, detects patterns of negative behavior from particular online players and sends them a quick message, gently letting them know they have crossed a line. "For neutral and positive players," Jeffrey Lin, a lead designer at Riot, told *GamesIndustry* magazine, "this subtle nudge is often enough to get them back on track."

Yet some hard-core bullies are unfazed by automated warnings and keep right on unloading their venom. In such cases, community members should step in—whether by writing a response to the aggressor on the forum or reporting bullying comments as abuse. When members of an online forum, discussion group or e-mail thread consistently refuse to tolerate bullying, new participants will probably conform to that established norm, turning the group into a force for good.

All online participants determine what a community's norms are. "If trolls show up, if the community as a whole can say, 'This is not something we want here,' it can convince that person to move on," Suler says. Taking a stand not only helps the victim but is also good for you: when people see others being bullied and fail to speak up, their own psychological health often suffers.

Concerned onlookers can also help curb bullying's spread by reaching out to victims individually via e-mail or direct message. Aggression often begets aggression–cyberbullying victims may turn around and bully others, according to San Diego State University psychologist Jean M. Twenge. But you can mitigate this effect by offering the abused your support and condemning the attacks. In a 2007 study Twenge and her colleagues found that when people made a short, friendly connection with someone else following an episode of social exclusion, the victim was less likely to show aggression afterward. "Having even one person accept you seemed to mitigate the [aggression] effect," says Twenge, author of *Generation Me*. "Reach out and say, 'I'm sorry this happened.'"

Such outreach is especially crucial because even antibullying education may not deter determined trolls. According to a 2013 study by University of Texas at Arlington criminologist Seokjin Jeong and Byung Hyun Lee of Michigan State University, students were more likely to be bullied at schools that had installed antibullying programs, perhaps because the programs inadvertently gave bullies ideas for tormenting their victims.

Rallying Friends

Many months after enduring online ridicule, Seida decided she was not going to let the bullies' vile comments define her. To give her detractors the middle finger, she did a boudoir photo shoot while wearing the now infamous Lara Croft costume. "If they're going to talk, I might as well give them something to talk about!" she says.

Seida's brush with cyberbullies inspired her to reach out to others on the receiving end of vicious online attacks. Along with a photographer friend, she created ifeeldelicious.com, a site designed to help victims of online bullying repair the damage to their dignity and psyche. She and other members ran a successful campaign against a notorious bully they called "the King of Mean," rallying others to boycott and speak out against his insult-ridden Web site and social media sites. She advises people who face relentless online jibes to gather a group of friends who appreciate them. Indeed, knowing someone else has your back goes a long way toward softening the impact of drive-by online attacks. "Talk to somebody–find a support system," Seida says. "If you keep it inside, it's just going to eat you alive."

What to Do If You're a Victim

If you have suffered abuse at the hands of cyberbullies, you are not alone. Millions of others have, too. Here are some expert-approved strategies to stop the harassment and minimize its effect on you.

—E.S.

Don't engage. When the harassment is relatively mild, the old "I can't hear you" approach really can work. Block the person's social media profile or just stop replying to the comments. The troll wants you to get worked up. When you don't respond, he or she sometimes loses interest.

Alert those in charge. Report abusive messages that include ad hominem attacks or vulgar language to someone who can make them stop—whether the police or an online forum's administrator. A 2014 survey found that in 61 percent of cases, social networks shut down reported harassers' accounts.

Talk to a professional. If online attacks are bad enough to make you seriously doubt your self-worth, consult a therapist. Cyberbullies are skilled at eliciting a very intense, instant reaction that may be unlike anything else you have experienced. You most likely will need support to deal with it.

About the Author

Elizabeth Svoboda is a science writer in San Jose, Calif., and author of What Makes a Hero? The Surprising Science of Selflessness *(Penguin Group, 2013).*

Section 3: How Smartphones Affect Mental and Physical Health

Social Notworking: Is Generation Smartphone Really More Prone to Unhappiness?

By Angus Chen

Mobile devices have become our alarm clocks and newspapers and, via platforms like Facebook and Instagram, portals to our social lives. With smartphones inhabiting the pockets of roughly three quarters of all Americans and tablets borne by half, a pale blue glow silhouettes modern life.

As screens have become ubiquitous, so has the phenomenon of depressed or suicidal teens, notes Jean Twenge, a psychologist at San Diego State University and the author of *iGen: Why Today's Super-Connected Kids Are Growing Up Less Rebellious, More Tolerant, Less Happy–and Completely Unprepared for Adulthood*.

In a study published in November in *Clinical Psychological Science*, Twenge correlates the increasing use of social media, gaming and Internet browsing with rising symptoms of depression and suicidal behaviors in teenagers. Importantly, however, other research has shown that some device use–on social media, in particular–might be positive for people struggling with depression or other serious mental illnesses.

The study led by Twenge collected data on more than half a million American teenagers' electronic device and online media habits from two national surveys conducted annually since 1991 and involving people ages 13 to 18. When Twenge compared those same teens' reports of having thoughts of or a plan to commit suicide–or making actual attempts–a third of teens who used devices at least two hours a day acknowledged at least one of these behaviors. That number went up to nearly half among teens who used devices for five or more hours a day. Teenagers who used social media on a daily basis were 13 percent more likely to say they felt depressed than were peers who did not use it every day.

Twenge and other researchers had been seeing dramatically rising rates of depression, especially among teens, over the past five years. "I noticed this very pronounced spike in depressive symptoms around 2012," she says. According to the data collected annually by the U.S. Centers for Disease Control and Prevention, the teen suicide rate has been climbing steadily since then, too.

One of the biggest things happening in society at exactly the time of the depression spike was a rapid proliferation of smartphones. "[It] was the year the percent of Americans who owned smartphones crossed 50 percent," Twenge says. By 2015 about 85 percent of young adults had smartphones and were using their devices a lot more, according to a Pew Research Center survey. "There was this turn where it wasn't just that people had smartphones," Twenge says. "It became the primary way teens communicated with one another."

For many teenagers, social media is not simply the primary medium of communication but the epicenter of social life itself. "If you don't have a Snapchat [account], you're not connected to anyone in school," says Aashima, a 16-year-old U.S. high school student. (Her surname is withheld to protect her privacy.)

Not only do students hear about gossip or drama more quickly as pictures and messages blaze through virtual networks; Aashima says social media won't let ugly rumors fade. "I remember in like fourth grade, we didn't really have cell phones and [gossip] would just die in school that day," she says. "But with texts and social media, you can discuss it when you're home, in the car–anytime." She adds people will bash each other online over something that happened in school or the way somebody looked one day. "And it just drags on and on and on," she says.

Social media also opens teens up to the worldwide online community. Aashima says strange men follow her accounts frequently and, as a courtesy, she often returns the favor. "And then they [direct message] me, and then they're like, 'What's up, girl?' And they just say really gross things. This morning I was dealing with someone like that. Like why do you have to take time out of your day to ask me these kinds of questions?" she says. "I feel like, in their eyes,

[I'm] another thing to use–to talk about. It's just really degrading." Despite her wariness, Aashima says she still wants to engage with people online. "Even if they're like the worst person ever," she says, "you just want everyone to like you and not think bad of you, so you try your best to do that. When that fails, you feel like giving up on yourself, and you just don't want to live anymore."

The uptick in teenage depression and suicidality has come almost entirely from young women, based on annual surveys of teenagers and young adults taken from 1991 to 2015 that are part of the University of Michigan's Monitoring the Future Series, which Twenge also used for her study. Some researchers say they can intuitively see possible reasons for this, although they are unsure of any definite factors. "Girls are very relational, so there's lots of detailed interactions around their relationships and who is doing what, who is more popular," says Holly Shakya, a psychologist at the University of California, San Diego, who did not work on Twenge's study.

Twenge also suggests smartphones' mere presence may affect physical and mental health. "There's blue light shining into your eyes and preventing you from feeling tired," she says. "They're also psychologically stimulating, and that can lead to you turning your thoughts over and over. In many cases it's 'Why didn't I get likes on that post?' or 'Is that other person doing something much more fun than me right now?'" These things can keep people up at night, and sleep-deprived people are more prone to depression, Twenge says.

But much of this is hard to prove, Shakya notes. For example, the new study did not address the question of whether gaming or social media use was more closely tied to depression. It merely correlated self-reported information on electronic device and social media use with suicidality and depression, which does not rule out the possibility that depressed people are likely to spend more time on social media.

Also, Twenge's study did not delve into exactly what people might have been doing when they were using their devices, says Kelly Aschbrenner, a mental health services researcher at the Geisel

School of Medicine at Dartmouth College, who was not involved with the work. The researchers "only ask how often they're using social media or devices. We don't know that people are scrolling through social media and viewing content that's upsetting them or interacting with others in a way that makes them feel bad," Aschbrenner says.

There are also significant reasons to believe social media can be healthful. "Our studies have shown people with mental health problems can benefit when they connect with others like them [on social media] to share advice [and] ailments and feel that they're not alone," Aschbrenner notes. "It's not like you can go to the park and scream out, 'Is anyone else feeling anxious today?' There are really few opportunities for people to find others in life who have the same stigmatized illness."

Aschbrenner says that although it is important to consider the risks of new technologies, health care providers and researchers should be leveraging social media and smartphones as a way to help people. "There are people with mental illnesses who are experiencing debilitating symptoms and can't leave their home," she says. "Social media could be a safe platform to help people connect with others as a first step."

Facebook, for one, says it shares that hope. The social network has wellness researchers who pay close attention to these findings and work to redesign the Web site's interface with healthiness in mind, according to a company representative. "We want people to be healthy users of social media and that includes connecting in a meaningful way with your friends and community on Facebook. This is something we think a lot about, and research is core to our efforts," Facebook's director of research, David Ginsberg, wrote in an e-mailed response to queries.

In some cases users should be mindful of ways technology might be hurting rather than helping them–but the crux of the matter is in how one uses it, Shakya says. Reaching out for support from friends on Facebook or even using the multitude of fitness or mental health apps may have significant benefits. "This isn't black and white," she says. "It's important to think about this stuff in nuance. It's not like social media is terrible and ruining the world."

Teenagers recognize this, too. "[The pros] are connecting to your friends immediately and being able to talk to them and share your ideas in a public way. If you want to say or advocate for something, it's easy to share to everyone, and people will see it," Aashima says. "It is very powerful. You can use it for good, and you can use it for bad."

School-Based Online Programs Instruct Pupils About Good Mental Health

By Shekhar Saxena and Anisha Padukone

Roughly 50 percent of all mental health conditions begin before people are in their mid-teens even though most go undetected and untreated. Adding to this, suicide is one of the top causes of death in young adults. The unprecedented disruptions of the pandemic has aggravated such problems, especially for younger age groups. All of these factors mean there is no better time to support and strengthen mental health education among teenagers.

In response to these needs, the World Health Organization has recently recommended several evidence-based interventions to protect and promote the mental health of adolescents by strengthening interpersonal and emotional regulation skills. A recent review of literature also suggests ways in which children and young people could be helped by the digital delivery of mental health interventions.

One of the most effective ways of implementing mental health education is through school systems, either as a course module within a class or as a separate class within the school. A lot of research has shown the effectiveness of these programs, but we need continued studies to further develop the best curricula to put in place to supplement existing social and educational programs.

The addition of technology and digitization will ensure more personalization, active participation and the ability to provide greater outreach at affordable costs. The Live Love Laugh Foundation, a mental health nonprofit organization in India, started an adolescent mental health program called You Are Not Alone in 2016. This program aims to educate adolescents and their teachers about stress, anxiety and depression. It also suggests tips to build resilience, provide access to support and normalize conversations about mental health within school settings.

So far, the program has educated more than 200,000 students and 20,000 teachers across the country. Results from a survey revealed that 76.6 percent of students had not attended a mental health awareness session previously. And 90 percent of the students, parents and teachers who responded from 32 schools across 10 Indian states were keen to have mental health sessions conducted. In the wake of the pandemic, this program is being digitized with an educational technology partner to cater to the vast number of Indian teens using a virtual learning platform. A facilitator delivers the session using a designated module while students learn and interact using quizzes, polls, and so on.

Another example is a program run by the Mental Health Association in New York State (MHANYS). In 2016 New York passed a law that made it mandatory for schools to provide mental health instruction as part of K–12 health education. The program offers a component to educate families and caregivers about youth mental health by providing access to webinars and other online resources to promote greater understanding of mental health and to support wellness for the whole family. It is intended to serve as a model for other cities and even for whole countries to follow.

The key factors that determine the success of a digital program are an entertaining design, a high level of interactivity for its users, an ability to reach large numbers of students across diverse regions, availability in numerous languages, and economic sustainability through low-cost or free access. These steps could enable a program to reach nearly two billion children globally, most of whom are in low- and middle-income countries.

To make these projects succeed, organizers must encourage public-private partnerships, collaborations with technology and social media companies, and recruitment of celebrities and other social icons as endorsers. If these elements all coalesce, we can create a revolution in mental health education for teens.

If You Need Help

If you or someone you know is struggling or having thoughts of suicide, help is available. Call the National Suicide Prevention Lifeline at 1-800-273-8255 (TALK), use the online Lifeline Chat or contact the Crisis Text Line by texting TALK to 741741.

This is an opinion and analysis article, and the views expressed by the author or authors are not necessarily those of Scientific American.

About the Authors

Shekhar Saxena is a professor of the practice of global mental health at the Harvard T. H. Chan School of Public Health. He is former director of mental health at the World Health Organization in Geneva.

Anisha Padukone is CEO of the Indian mental health nonprofit The Live Love Laugh Foundation.

Texting Thumb, Trigger Finger, Gamer's Thumb and Other Smartphone Injuries

By Carolyn Barber

As a longtime emergency department physician, I have a case study I'd like to share with you. The patient's right thumb knuckle is inflamed, swollen and often painful, especially toward the end of the day, and the inside part is a little numb. Her grip is slightly weakened, and her palm aches. Her middle finger intermittently has a new "catch" to it when bent. The second and third fingers are slightly swollen.

I'll get to the diagnosis in just a moment. For now, let me just say that this is a patient I know quite well–so well, in fact, that I'm not sure how I didn't see this coming.

For a decade, I have used my smartphone to hammer out voluminous emergency medicine reports that highlight various medical conditions, which I then share with a broad array of doctors each week, the better to stay on top of important trends and topics in our field. Then came the pandemic, which ratcheted up my phone game to staggering new levels.

I followed top scientists on Twitter, pored over COVID-19 literature, ordered goods and services, caught up with breaking news, messaged friends, wrote e-mails, composed longer notes and full letters, and of course produced those long reports. I swiped up, highlighted, bolded, copied, pasted, collated–all of it on a mobile device that fits in one hand, albeit awkwardly.

So yes, the patient is me. And yes, my dominant hand has taken a beating. Swelling in my index and long fingers–my swiping fingers–is affecting my ability to fully close my fist. Additionally, my long finger is catching some when I bend it. It becomes stuck sometimes when bent and then straightens with a snap.

Score: Technology 1, User 0.

"You are not alone," Jeffrey Stone assures me. Stone, an upper extremity surgeon at the Florida Orthopedic Institute, says he has long seen these injuries from texting, computer work, gaming, doctors recording information online, surgeons holding retractors or forceps, and so on. "But now it's everybody," he says, "because people are constantly between their phones, [electronic] pads and computers. They're constantly banging away."

"Texting thumb," which you may also hear called "smartphone thumb," may not be an official medical diagnosis. But it is a real phenomenon, if somewhat ill-defined, and stems from overuse and subsequent inflammation. Trigger thumb (or trigger finger), which some providers are beginning to associate with phone users who constantly swipe and text, is another real thing. We are dwelling here within the broader category of repetitive stress injuries, which may occur in any body part being asked to do the same thing repeatedly. And when I say "we," I mean it.

"Texting thumb is a way for me to say to somebody, 'It appears to me that you're doing too much of this,'" says Stone. "It's a garbage can all-inclusive term to say, 'It appears that the biggest culprit to this continuing to be a problem for you–and continuing to inhibit your life–is the amount of time you're spending texting.'"

As John Erickson, a hand and upper extremity surgeon at the Raleigh Hand to Shoulder Center, tells me, "Ergonomically, smartphones weren't designed with the hands and wrists in mind." Stone says smartphone users are "running marathons with their thumbs every day," and because the joints are very small in your hands, the amount of force transmitted is tremendous. Stone says that one pound of pressure at the tip of the thumb can translate to about 12 to 14 pounds of pressure at the base of the thumb joint.

"I consider texting thumb as more of a repetitive stress injury," says David Bozentka, chief of hand surgery at the University of Pennsylvania. High-velocity texting, hands held in awkward positions, fingers stretched to reach faraway keys–all of these contribute to the problem alongside other predisposing factors, experts say.

Trigger finger occurs when the flexor tendon becomes thickened and inflamed inside a narrow tunnel, or sheath, sometimes causing the finger to be stuck in a bent position. It is often seen in people who use their hands for repetitive movements, such as frequent gripping or pinching, or after forceful use of the fingers and thumb. Sound familiar?

In my own case, I've developed inflammation and mild arthritis in my right thumb metacarpal joint, which my doctor and I suspect was exacerbated by excessive smartphone use. The pain and the degenerative arthritic changes are present only in my right (texting) thumb, which is significantly larger than my left thumb. The pain resolves completely at night after resting it, but recurs the next day when I resume pecking and swiping–and I do resume.

Multiple studies have shown the cumulative effects of smartphone use on the musculoskeletal system, with up to two thirds of mobile device users in one study having such complaints, associated with the frequency of making phone calls, texting and gaming. Another study found the highest prevalence of complaints in the upper neck, back, and wrists and hands.

Let's face it: our hands weren't really made for all of this. Experts describe another painful tendonitis at the thumb base called "gamer's thumb" or De Quervain's disease. It seems to be associated with frequent texting on smartphones or gaming, among other causes, though more research is needed. At a more anatomical level, ultrasound studies have shown thickening and changes in thumb tendons of frequent texters–and the thickness paralleled the numbers of messages per day.

"And there's other smartphone overuse injuries that we see," says Brandon Donnelly, a hand surgeon with Pontchartrain Orthopedics and Sports Medicine in Metairie, La. "'Text claw,' or pain and cramping in the fingers, is one along with carpal tunnel and 'cell phone elbow,' which is caused by prolonged bending. Users may bend their wrist or elbow while watching the latest viral video, streaming television and scrolling through social media content,"

Donnelly says. Experts agree that more research is needed to better understand and detail technology's role in all of these conditions.

"I advise people to at least put their phone on the table when they can," says Stone. "The mere act of holding it involves gripping it with your thumb and small finger, so your intrinsic muscles are straining and your palm hurts." As you've no doubt noticed, they're making many smartphones bigger, not smaller. That's an issue, especially for someone with smaller hands.

Smartphone addiction has been increasing worldwide, particularly among young adults, and those age groups are not immune from injury. "It's not like an epidemic, but it's certainly a steady flow of these kinds of patients coming in," says Erickson.

Most cases of texting thumb can be treated conservatively by simply resting the thumb. Given the trend toward more phone use, that's easier said than done. Still, Erickson says, "The most obvious thing is activity modification."

Try some of these measures to give your thumb a break: Use your index finger or different fingers to text and swipe. Employ voice recognition software on devices when possible. Use a desktop or laptop when composing longer notes. Limit gaming time. Consider anti-inflammatory medication, if not contraindicated.

For the overwhelming majority of high-tech sufferers, such conservative actions should do the trick. Erickson says that if things aren't improving in a few weeks, one should seek medical attention. That may mean a thumb brace or splint, oral or topical nonsteroidal medications, hand therapy, referral to occupational therapy, and perhaps a cortisone shot. In my case, I'm hoping that a recent steroid injection will reduce the inflammation and swelling in my trigger finger. My hand surgeon estimates that the treatment is effective in roughly 70 percent of cases. Occasionally, surgery is necessary for recalcitrant conditions.

Physician awareness will be important going forward. We sometimes diagnose conditions and treat patients without fully considering the cause–which, in this case, is nearly completely reversible once corrective measures are taken. I suspect we underdiagnose smartphone use as at least an important contributor to various repetitive stress injuries. In 20 years in the ER, I can tell you this etiology for various musculoskeletal complaints never crossed my mind. I simply didn't know. I do now.

More broadly, it's probably wise for all of us to spend a little more time unplugged. (Guilty as charged, over here.) Take a walk. Pocket your phone. And give your tweeting digits the break they deserve.

About the Author

Carolyn Barber has been an emergency department physician for 25 years. She is co-founder of the homeless work program Wheels of Change and author of many articles and the book Runaway Medicine: What You Don't Know May Kill You, *which was recently Amazon's number-one Hot New Release in Health Care Administration. She received her M.D. at the Johns Hopkins University School of Medicine.*

The Double-Edged Sword of Technology for LGBTQ+ Teens

By Danielle Ramo

To be young and LGBTQ+ in 2020 America means living in a culture of both remarkable progress and pervasive challenges. Same-sex marriage is legal; there's an increasing number of positive, identity-affirming sexual and gender minority characters in movies and television; celebrities and influencers are out and proud on social media; and many of us are living thriving lives as out professionals, parents and members of the community.

Yet many LGBTQ+ youth continue to face discrimination and denial of their right to express their identity and are still facing unique and emerging mental health challenges in a locked-down era of COVID. As national attention is rightly on racial injustices, and pride celebrations this year focus on the solidarity of the racial and sexual and gender minority movements, there is no better time to focus on how technology can be used to promote justice and supportive community for LGBTQ+ young people.

LGBTQ+ teens still experience mental health challenges at alarmingly high rates compared to our straight, cisgender counterparts. A national survey by the Trevor project found that 39 percent of LGBTQ+ youth had seriously considered suicide in the past year, and the CDC estimates rates of suicidality among LGB youth to be between three and five times that of their straight peers. Young LGBTQ+ Black, Indigenous and People of Color (BIPOC) are at unique risk of experiencing multiple forms of discrimination and aggression (based on the intersectionality of minority identities), that make them particularly susceptible to chronic stress and mental health challenges.

These disparities are particularly acute among transgender and gender non-binary youth. Although coming out as trans or gender non-binary (identifying other than male or female) is increasingly common, discrimination and violence toward youth who identify this way are still rampant. The U.S. Transgender Survey found that 40 percent of transgender adults in America report at least one suicide attempt in their lives (nearly nine times the national average), and 73 percent of those who had attempted suicide did so for the first time when they were under the age of 18. In Black trans or gender non-binary youth, thoughts of suicide and suicide attempts are twice as high as cisgender Black LGBQ youth. While sheltered in place during COVID-19, LGBTQ+ teens may be confined with people who don't accept them, forcing them back in the closet, back to an identity that does not reflect their reality, and in some cases they may be physically or mentally unsafe. This is even more likely for BIPOC, whose families may not be accepting of their LGBTQ+ identity. The psychological ramifications of this are likely to be deep and long-lasting.

Technology can be a lifeline for many. Adolescents and young adults today have unprecedented access to online information and communities; 95 percent of American teens have a smartphone (or access to one), and 45 percent say they are online "almost constantly." This generation of LGBTQ+ adolescents often relies on connections made with technology for social support and identity-building, as well as accessing vital information and resources. A national survey of teens and young adults conducted by Hopelab and Wellbeing Trust showed that LGBTQ+ teens are more likely than others to seek out information about depression, anxiety, stress and other mental health issues online. Virtual spaces offer safety and support that may not be available in their offline lives, through providing a space to engage as their authentic selves, often for the first time.

But it's complicated, and the internet is not necessarily a safe place. Many LGBTQ+ teens are exposed to abuse online. Harassment and cyberbullying are common for LGBTQ+ teens, who are less likely than others to seek help when it happens–and it is doubly rampant for BIPOC young people. Online harassment is nothing new, but this is different. Minority stress theory helps us understand how experiences and expectations of sexuality-, gender-, and ethnicity-based discrimination create a stress experience unique to people with minority status in society and fuel a range of harmful cognitive states associated with depression, anxiety and suicidality.

As LGBTQ+ young people shelter in place and thus are more likely to be online, this duality of risk and promise is particularly dangerous. Experiencing rejection and abuse at exactly the moment and in exactly the places where young people are seeking refuge can be devastating, and may result in more negative mental health outcomes than we can currently predict.

How can we navigate the double-edged sword of technology for LGBTQ+ teens? In response to COVID, there has been a groundswell of digital services supporting well-being and delivering psychiatric or psychological support to those who need it, but very few of these services are tailored to the emotional and cultural experiences of LGBTQ+ teens, and almost none for BIPOC. LGBTQ+ individuals and people of color consistently report a preference for mental health interventions that are tailored for them. There needs to be a wider offering of support that LGBTQ+ teens experience as safe, comfortable, and culturally appropriate, especially for those who are BIPOC.

The Born This Way Foundation, the Trevor Project, the It Gets Better Project, and media outlets such as Them, for example, provide foundational support to build affirming ideas of the LGBTQ+ experience, strategies to deal with stress, and immediate help in times of crisis. And critically, LGBTQ+ tailored interventions may be more likely to work: in a clinical trial I published with colleagues in *Nicotine and Tobacco Research* late last year, we showed that an online smoking cessation program tailored to the experience of LGBTQ+ young adults was more effective at helping them quit than one targeted more broadly.

The need for online mental health services tailored to serve LGBTQ+ youth, especially transgender, gender non-binary, and BIPOC youth, is critical in this moment, as their needs are heightened; access to support is limited and the dangers are complex; and the potential for harm is profound. Right now, tech and behavioral science hold the potential to meet that need. They're here, they're queer, and we have to get used to reaching them where they are, which is online.

The views expressed are those of the author(s) and are not necessarily those of Scientific American.

About the Author

Danielle Ramo, Ph.D., is a clinical psychologist and senior director of research at Hopelab, a social innovation laboratory that builds behavior change tech to improve the lives of teens and young adults. She is also an adjunct associate professor of psychiatry at the University of California, San Francisco, leading a research program at the intersection of substance use and digital mental health. She regularly writes and speaks about teen mental health in the digital age. She lives in San Francisco with her spouse and three children.

Mining Social Media Reveals Mental Health Trends and Helps Prevent Self-Harm

By Rotem Kopel

Globally, more than four billion people use social media, generating huge stores of data from their devices. That information can be used in tracking more than just what they buy, their political leanings or the patterns of social media usage during the pandemic. It can also be channeled to help better detect mental illness and improve well-being.

A growing number of studies show that language patterns and images in posts can reveal and predict mental health conditions for individuals and also evaluate mental health trends across entire populations.

Thanks to advances in artificial intelligence, natural language processing and other data science tools, researchers, tech companies, government agencies and nongovernmental organizations can make use of these gargantuan databases to look for signs of mental health conditions, such as depression, anxiety and suicide risk.

In certain countries, Facebook's online suicide prevention program uses AI to scan users' posts for images and words that may identify a person who may have a tendency toward self-harm. A team of trained human reviewers is alerted to posts that display patterns of suicidal thoughts and sends out mental health resources to at-risk users. In serious cases, emergency services may be notified to warn of imminent risk for self-harm.

Pinterest's "compassionate search" connects users seeking information on anxiety and other mental-health-related topics with links that promote emotional wellness, including deep-breathing activities and more elaborate psychotherapy exercises. And Snapchat has developed the Here For You in-app support feature to help users who may be experiencing mental health challenges. One of the main functions monitors search terms related to mental health conditions and then provides users with links to helpful resources and a direct link to a help hotline.

In addition to tech companies, several countries have also started to address mental health issues through social media channels. In 2018 Canada launched a pilot to analyze random social media data to identify geographical suicide hotspots, which enabled an appropriate allocation of resources.

A number of research organizations are also using social media data to develop real-time observation tools that could be used by policy makers. The tools analyze well-being indicators such as happiness, other sentiments and signs of mental health issues. Researchers have recently demonstrated that depression indexes correlate with geographical and demographic patterns, as reported by the U.S. Centers for Disease Control and Prevention. During the COVID-19 pandemic, when traditional survey methods failed to provide results fast enough, researchers used positive and negative mood indicators to rapidly assess population status.

Using AI algorithms to analyze moods and mental health conditions through social media posts is in its infancy. Still, it is not too early to address technical, ethical, cultural and social questions. There may be a desire to detect mental health conditions based solely on social media information–for example, via a hashtag such as #depression–rather than on an actual clinical verification of a person's condition. Researchers, moreover, may have difficulty extracting data easily from most social media platforms, so the scope of what they find may be limited. Tech companies may develop detection and prediction algorithms of mental health indicators but do so without publishing their work in academic journals or having it reviewed by panels of independent experts.

Before data mining of social media proceeds further, a number of questions need to be addressed. How can patterns of word usage on social media be connected to clinically rigorous definitions for mental health? Do algorithms for self-harm detection need to be validated by the research community? How can users' privacy and their mental health data be secured?

The numerous questions and challenges do not undermine an unprecedented opportunity to further develop the frameworks and tools necessary to harness technology to benefit mental health. Self-harm detection incorporated into social media could save lives because people at risk often do not approach family members or professionals. Mental health indexes derived from social media can also serve as tools to shape public health policies because they allow for rapid assessment of new initiatives' impact in real time and the identification of at-risk subpopulations.

Bringing similar ideas into widespread use will require public-private partnerships to help researchers access data, allow AI algorithms to become more transparent, promote collaborative innovation and ultimately bring about better technological solutions for managing public and individual mental health.

If You Need Help

If you or someone you know is struggling or having thoughts of suicide, help is available. Call the National Suicide Prevention Lifeline at 1-800-273-8255 (TALK), use the online Lifeline Chat or contact the Crisis Text Line by texting TALK to 741741.

This is an opinion and analysis article, and the views expressed by the author or authors are not necessarily those of Scientific American.

About the Author

Rotem Kopel is CEO of MindMatters, a philanthropic foundation based in Geneva.

Green with Facebook Envy, Red with Twitter Rage

By Tori Rodriguez and Maggie Puniewska

Spending a lot of time on Facebook is linked to diminished well-being, according to many studies. Yet questions linger about cause and effect–perhaps people who are already lonely simply spend more time on social media. New studies reveal that Facebook can indeed affect mood and mental state, and whether the effect is positive or negative depends heavily on how a person interacts with his or her contacts. Several of the new findings reveal that when Facebook hurts, the underlying culprit is–you guessed it–envy.

A study published in February 2015 in *Computers in Human Behavior* surveyed 736 college students and found that when Facebook evoked envy, it increased symptoms of depression. But a March 2015 study from the same journal found that Facebook use can also decrease depression if users sign on seeking social connection and support and then feel they have received it.

Those studies did not attempt to figure out why some people experienced envy and others did not but others have found that the way a user interacts with Facebook may be crucial. For example, researchers at the University of Michigan and the University of Leuven in Belgium tracked 173 students' habits over time and found that passive use–browsing news feeds, for example–led to reduced well-being by increasing feelings of envy. Active use, such as posting and commenting, had no such effect, according to the two studies, published in April 2015 in the *Journal of Experimental Psychology: General*.

Another important factor seems to be how close you are to the people with whom you interact. Two related experiments published in November 2015 in *Computers in Human Behavior* were the first to explore the role of relationship strength in users' emotional responses to posts on the site. Among a sample of 207 American adults and 194 German college students, the researchers found that people more often felt positive emotions than negative ones when browsing the site, and their emotions were amplified when reading posts from someone they knew well. "Empathy is more pronounced when the relationship is closer, so one is more likely to 'catch' the happiness of a close friend than a casual acquaintance," says study co-author Ruoyun Lin, a doctoral student at the Leibniz Institute's Knowledge Media Research Center in Tübingen, Germany. Close friends can inspire envy, too, but the researchers found that this type of envy tended to be benign—the overall reaction to a friend's good news was usually positive.

The takeaway, the experts say, is that you can control how Facebook makes you feel. If you tend to compare yourself with others or get envious easily, you might consider limiting your time spent on social networking sites or make a conscious effort to use them in active rather than passive ways. "Our findings show the importance of human agency," says Edson Tandoc, Jr., co-author of the February 2015 study and assistant professor in the Division of Journalism and Publishing at Nanyang Technological University in Singapore. "It is not technology such as Facebook that affects our feelings per se but rather how we use it."

—Tori Rodriguez

People who rant online may have offline rage, too

Releasing pent-up anger can be very healing, so it is no surprise that in this tech-dominated age more of us are turning to the Internet to air our grievances. In fact, 46 percent of Twitter users said they tweet as a way to deal with anger and 37 percent hoped that the person or group they vented about would see their online commentary, according to data collected by Ryan Martin, a psychologist at the University of Wisconsin–Green Bay. In the short term this "e-anger" may feel cathartic: a study published in *Cyberpsychology, Behavior and Social Networking* by Martin and his colleagues in 2013 found that 100 percent of the 24 participants who ranted online said they felt calm and relaxed afterward.

Yet unleashing frustrations in the digital space is not always healthy. The study had participants fill out a survey, which measured their tendency to experience anger, how they expressed it and any consequences related to it. Researchers found that people who had ranted online were not only more irritable than the average person, they also experienced more consequences of anger offline, averaging one physical and two verbal fights a month. Whether or not posting fiery comments makes you more aggressive is unclear but Martin believes that "the more you vent through social media, the more likely you are to utilize negative expression styles in other areas of your life and vice versa." Our digital and "real-life" selves can feed off each other.

–Maggie Puniewska

Kids Are Not Hurt by Screen Time

By Jared Rizzi

Kids spend a lot of time looking at screens. And some parents worry. But a new study argues against the apprehension parents may feel.

"The danger is that they're hearing a message that social media, digital technology use is causing very serious and harmful problems like depression, like suicide-related behaviors."

Candice Odgers, professor of psychological science at the University of California, Irvine.

"And the idea is that if you shut off social media, which lots of kids use to connect with each other, their friends, find out information about health, you could be making a situation worse. Parents are really being sent a message that is not supported by anything scientifically."

Odgers and her colleagues looked at the screen-related behavior of 400 public-school students in North Carolina ages 10 to 14. This group was picked as a representative sample of race and socioeconomic status for the entire U.S. The researchers found that—even not counting time doing schoolwork on screens—the kids spent between almost five hours to seven hours per day on their devices, with the older kids online the most. That's a lot of hours, but:

"Overall, what we find is no connection between the amount of time that young people spend online using digital technologies and mental health symptoms like depression, anxiety. When we do find associations, they were actually quite surprising to us. We found that young people who sent more text messages actually reported better mental health. Now, again, this was a small association, but it reflects what other people have found: that people who are very connected off-line, that use technology in the positive ways to stay connected often, are more connected online as well and experiencing better mental health."

The new study is in the journal *Clinical Psychological Science*. [Michaeline Jensen et al., Young adolescents' digital technology use and mental health symptoms: little evidence of longitudinal or daily linkages]

So why the fears about screen time? Odgers argues that the methodologies for older studies may have led to false conclusions.

"One of the issues with the research that's been done to date has been that youth are, you know, in school. They have a survey put in front of them, and they're asked to recall, over the past six months, 'How often are you online?' and 'Have you ever felt depressed?' And the correlation between those two things has been used to spread a lot of fear around this connection between social media use and things like depression–99.5 percent of the reasons that kids differ in their depression is due to something other than the time they spend online."

Parents get a lot of advice, and some of it always seems to conflict. But Odgers suggests there's one place you can always go to get information.

"The hope is that more parents will hear this message and relax and spend kind of less time worrying about smartphones and more time just talking to their kids."

–Jared Rizzi

[The above text is a transcript of this podcast.]

How Consumers and Health Care Providers Can Judge the Quality of Digital Mental Health Tools

By Ian Hickie and Cameron Fox

More than 10,000 apps in the Apple and Google Play stores claim to treat psychological difficulties, and the list doesn't stop with downloads for your smartphone. Wearables, artificial intelligence software, augmented and virtual reality, and video games all have arrived to address mental health needs in creative ways.

To be sure, those needs are great. "The global burden of disease attributable to mental disorders has risen inexorably in all countries in the context of major demographic, environmental, and socio-political transitions," noted the Lancet Commission on Global Mental Health and Sustainable Development in 2018. The pandemic, moreover, is a portent of a "second epidemic" of mental ill-health sweeping the world.

Digital mental health solutions have increased in appeal as in-person care has been seriously compromised in a socially isolated world. Benefits in the form of improved access and affordability for consumers, personal control over the learning experience and real-time feedback have drawn the notice of governments, insurance bodies, employers and others who wish to procure these products and services on behalf of those in need.

With the huge variety of solutions has come a set of quality-control problems. An immediate question arises for any product: Which digital tools have been designed based on the best clinical evidence, and which have been tested to ensure that they provide substantive benefit to patients?

This is where the power of "soft standards" and regulation comes into play: several organizations, such as OneMind, Health Navigator and the World Economic Forum, have begun developing assessment criteria for digital mental-health tools. These measurements will allow innovators to receive a stamp of approval that a product is clinically validated, ethical, secure and effective. We predict that such mechanisms will benefit the emerging ecosystem for these types of products. Procurement bodies, both public and private, can then be assured that the products they purchase deliver as promised.

Standards will ensure that quality is considered as early as possible in the product design process. Companies will have a target to aim for to receive a stamp of approval to stay competitive, making them eager to stand out from the crowd and "show their work," as a recent STAT News article put it. Most important, consumers can trust that the product or service meets a minimum standards.

Given the impacts of the pandemic, the global sense of urgency is clear. Innovative companies promote the benefits of their products and services directly to consumers and to the insurers and other third-party providers who ultimately pay the bills. The need to promote an appropriate set of "marketplace" standards remains a priority as companies sell their products across international boundaries. As Yuri Marichich, chief medical officer of Pear Therapeutics, said in the STAT News article, "There's a huge opportunity here to be able to help patients if we do things right. But trust with patients is so important, trust with health care providers and also payers is so important. And you can't have trust if you are trying to circumvent doing the right thing."

This is an opinion and analysis article, and the views expressed by the author or authors are not necessarily those of Scientific American.

About the Authors

Ian Hickie is a professor of psychiatry and the co-director of health and policy at the Brain and Mind Center at the University of Sydney. He has led major public health and health services developments in Australia, particularly focusing on early intervention for young people with depression, suicidal thoughts and behaviors, and complex mood disorders. Through co-design, implementation and continuous evaluation, Hickie is active in the development of new health information and personal monitoring technologies to drive highly personalized and measurement-based care. He is a 5 percent shareholder in InnoWell Pty Ltd. (the joint venture of PwC Australia and the University of Sydney).

Cameron Fox works on the World Economic Forum's Platform for Shaping the Future of Health and Healthcare, where he manages the Global Future Council on Mental Health in addition to a portfolio of projects touching on the future of digital solutions and technology for health care. Previously, Cameron was a Bass Connections fellow at Duke University, where he focused on the ethical, legal and social implications of advances in neuroscience and genetics. He has a background in neuroscience and philosophy.

Section 4: Smartphones and the Sharing of Information and Opinions

Welcome to the Ultimate Neuroscience Lab: Your Smartphone

By Karen Rommelfanger and Álvaro Fernández Ibáñez

Back in 2013, a seminal U.N. report highlighted that more people have mobile phones than flush toilets. Today we can leverage smartphones and wearables to create more representative data pools of our global population than studies done with WEIRD (western, educated, industrialized, rich and democratic) research participants—in other words, typical U.S. college students.

Also, can you guesstimate how many times the average person touches a cell phone in a day? The answer is approximately 3,000 times.

A rich tapestry of our lives can increasingly be woven together by aggregating and analyzing each touch—and each conversation, oral or written, held by billions of people, every day.

Such data have already proved invaluable in bridging dozens if not hundreds of research gaps by collecting real-world, "ecologically valid" information from people in their natural day-to-day lives rather than in the artificial environment of a typical lab. Further, the information can help us bring objective, quantitative data down the line to psychology and psychiatry researchers. Most research still attempts to quantify assessments of mental illnesses, such as depression, based on patients' biased subjective reporting.

Neuroscientists and technologists are hard at work developing earlier and more accurate diagnoses for a variety of disorders, as well as personalized therapies for patients and preventive interventions for the general public. The data can be acquired through active means (what you type) and passive observations (how you type). All of this research can be conducted using inexpensive sensors embedded in smartphones and other personal devices.

Once this wealth of data is at hand, machine learning and artificial intelligence will offer opportunities to quickly analyze massive data sets acquired from these sensors to formulate diagnoses, develop treatment regimens and even make predictions about the risk of mental health issues for both individuals and the community as a whole.

Given that biological markers and diagnostic criteria for mental health conditions remain sparse and unclear, the rhythm and patterns discerned from the data gathered offers a quantitative window on mental health. The ultimate goal is to offer universal access to accurate diagnoses and timely, effective, personalized therapies to the planet's eight billion human minds.

Digital technologies are beginning to revive the sleepy field of psychiatry. We can utilize commercial-grade technologies and data sets and help apply these findings into health care practice much faster than the typical lag time of 17 years. In a nutshell, digital psychiatry can democratize applied research as citizens choose to use apps to self-manage their mental health and self-care and consent to share their data with researchers and digital developers.

While there is enormous opportunity, we also see thorny ethical issues. Who will have access to the data, and for what purpose? App and device users do not always know what data they are sharing and with whom. Developers, ethicists, citizens and policy makers must find practical resolutions as to how to manage trade-offs for benefits and risks, data protection and privacy, the accuracy of the underlying algorithms for machine learning and artificial intelligence, informed consent protocols, and more.

But the opportunity is real. Every smartphone is a lab, and every smartphone user is a scientist in the making.

This is an opinion and analysis article, and the views expressed by the author or authors are not necessarily those of Scientific American.

About the Authors

Karen Rommelfanger is a neuroscientist, neurotech ethicist and strategist. She directs the Neuroethics and Neurotechnology Innovation Collaboratory, which is characterized as a "think-and-do tank." At Emory University, she is an associate professor in the departments of neurology and psychiatry and director of the Emory Center for Ethics' neuroethics program.

Álvaro Fernández Ibáñez runs SharpBrains, an independent market research firm tracking applied neuroscience and digital technologies. He serves on the advisory boards of the Global Teacher Prize and SEK Education Group, and he co-authored The SharpBrains Guide to Brain Fitness *and the Spanish-language book* El Cerebro Que Cura.

Schoolkids Are Falling Victim to Disinformation and Conspiracy Fantasies

By Melinda Wenner Moyer

When Amanda Gardner, an educator with two decades of experience, helped to start a new charter elementary and middle school outside of Seattle last year, she did not anticipate teaching students who denied that the Holocaust happened, argued that COVID is a hoax and told their teacher that the 2020 presidential election was rigged. Yet some children insisted that these conspiracy fantasies were true. Both misinformation, which includes honest mistakes, and disinformation, which involves an intention to mislead, have had "a growing impact on students over the past 10 to 20 years," Gardner says, yet many schools do not focus on the issue. "Most high schools probably do some teaching to prevent plagiarism, but I think that's about it."

Children, it turns out, are ripe targets for fake news. Age 14 is when kids often start believing in unproven conspiratorial ideas, according to a study published in September 2021 in the *British Journal of Developmental Psychology*. Many teens also have trouble assessing the credibility of online information. In a 2016 study involving nearly 8,000 U.S. students, Stanford University researchers found that more than 80 percent of middle schoolers believed that an advertisement labeled as sponsored content was actually a news story. The researchers also found that less than 20 percent of high schoolers seriously questioned spurious claims in social media, such as a Facebook post that said images of strange-looking flowers, supposedly near the site of a nuclear power plant accident in Japan, proved that dangerous radiation levels persisted in the area. When college students in the survey looked at a Twitter post touting a poll favoring gun control, more than two thirds failed to note that the liberal antigun groups behind the poll could have influenced the data.

Disinformation campaigns often directly go after young users, steering them toward misleading content. A 2018 *Wall Street Journal* investigation found that YouTube's recommendation algorithm, which offers personalized suggestions about what users should watch next, is skewed to recommend videos that are more extreme and far-fetched than what the viewer started with. For instance, when researchers searched for videos using the phrase "lunar eclipse," they were steered to a video suggesting that Earth is flat. YouTube is one of the most popular social media site among teens: After Zeynep Tufekci, an associate professor at the University of North Carolina, Chapel Hill, School of Information and Library Science, spent time searching for videos on YouTube and observed what the algorithm told her to watch next, she suggested that it was "one of the most powerful radicalizing instruments of the 21st century."

One tool that schools can use to deal with this problem is called media literacy education. The idea is to teach kids how to evaluate and think critically about the messages they receive and to recognize falsehoods masquerading as truth. For children whose parents might believe conspiracy fantasies or other lies fueled by disinformation, school is the one place where they can be taught skills to evaluate such claims objectively.

Yet few American kids are receiving this instruction. Last summer Illinois became the first U.S. state to require all high school students to take a media literacy class. Thirteen other states have laws that touch on media literacy, but requirements can be as general as putting a list of resources on an education department Web site. A growing number of students are being taught some form of media literacy in college, but that is "way, way too late to begin this kind of instruction," says Howard Schneider, executive director of the Center for News Literacy at Stony Brook University. When he began teaching college students years ago, he found that "they came with tremendous deficits, and they were already falling into very bad habits."

Even if more students took such classes, there is profound disagreement about what those courses should teach. Certain curricula try to train students to give more weight to journalistic sources, but some researchers argue that this practice ignores the potential biases of publications and reporters. Other courses push students to identify where information comes from and ask how the content helps those disseminating it. Overall there are very few data showing the best way to teach children how to tell fact from fiction.

Most media literacy approaches "begin to look thin when you ask, 'Can you show me the evidence?'" says Sam Wineburg, a professor of education at Stanford University, who runs the Stanford History Education Group. There are factions of educational researchers behind each method, says Renee Hobbs, director of the Media Education Lab at the University of Rhode Island, and "each group goes out of its way to diss the other." These approaches have not been compared head-to-head, and some have only small studies supporting them. Like online media sources themselves, it is hard to know which ones to trust.

News literacy is a subset of media literacy research that deals directly with the propagation of conspiracies and the ability to discern real news from fake stories. It entails a set of skills that help people judge the reliability and credibility of news and information. But as with media literacy, researchers have very different ideas about how this type of news analysis should be taught.

Some programs, such as Schneider's Stony Brook program and the nonprofit, Washington, D.C.–based News Literacy Project, teach students to discern the quality of the information in part by learning how responsible journalism works. They study how journalists pursue news, how to distinguish between different kinds of information and how to judge evidence behind reported stories. The goal, Schneider wrote in a 2007 article for *Nieman Reports*, is to shape students into "consumers who could differentiate between raw, unmediated information coursing through the Internet and independent, verified journalism."

Yet some media literacy scholars doubt the efficacy of these approaches. Hobbs, for instance, wrote a 2010 paper arguing that these methods glorify journalism, ignore its many problems and do little to instill critical thinking skills. "All that focus on the ideals of journalism is mere propaganda if it is blind to the realities of contemporary journalism, where partisan politics and smear fests are the surest way to build audiences," she stated.

Other approaches teach students methods for evaluating the credibility of news and information sources, in part by determining the goals and incentives of those sources. They teach students to ask: Who created the content and why? And what do other sources say? But these methods are relatively new and have not been widely studied.

The lack of rigorous studies of the different approaches is indeed a major roadblock, says Paul Mihailidis, a civic media and journalism expert at Emerson College. He is the principal investigator of the Mapping Impactful Media Literacy Practices initiative, a research project supported by the National Association for Media Literacy Education. "Most of the science done is very small scale, very exploratory. It's very qualitative," he says. That is not simply because of a lack of resources, he adds. "There's also a lack of clarity about what the goals are."

For instance, in a 2017 study researchers looked at how well students who had taken Stony Brook's undergraduate course could answer certain questions a year later compared with students who had not. Students who had taken the class were more likely to correctly answer questions about the news media, such as that PBS does not rely primarily on advertising for financial support. But the study did not test how well the students could discern fake from real news, so it is hard to know how well the program inoculates students against falsehoods.

Moreover, the small amount of research that does exist has largely been conducted with college students, not the middle school or high school students who are so vulnerable to disinformation. Indeed, the various approaches that are being used in K–12 classrooms have hardly been tested at all. As part of his current research initiative, Mihailidis and his team interviewed the heads of all major organizations that are part of the National Media Literacy Alliance, which works to promote media literacy education. "We are finding, repeatedly, that many of the ways in which they support schools and teachers–resources, guidelines, best practices, etcetera–are not studied in much of a rigorous fashion," he says.

Some researchers, including Wineburg, are trying to fill in the research gaps. In a study published in 2019, Wineburg and his team compared how 10 history professors, 10 journalism fact-checkers and 25 Stanford undergraduates evaluated Web sites and information on social and political issues. They found that whereas historians and students were often fooled by manipulative Web sites, journalism fact-checkers were not. In addition, their methods of analysis differed significantly: historians and students tried to assess the validity of Web sites and information by reading vertically, navigating within a site to learn more about it, but fact-checkers read laterally, opening new browser tabs for different sources and running searches to judge the original Web site's credibility.

Working with the Poynter Institute and the Local Media Association and with support from Google.org (a charity founded by the technology giant), Wineburg and his team have created a civic online reasoning course that teaches students to evaluate information by reading laterally. The effects so far look promising. In a field experiment involving 40,000 high school students in urban public health districts, Wineburg and his group found that students who took the class became better able to evaluate Web sites and the credibility of online claims, such as Facebook posts, compared with students who did not take the class.

Still, even if news literacy education teaches specific skills well, some researchers question its broader, longer-term impact. Once students learn how to evaluate Web sites and claims, how confident can we be that they will retain these skills and use them down the line? How sure can we be that these methods will inculcate students with skepticism about conspiracy theories and disinformation campaigns? And will these methods lead students to become civically engaged members of society? "There's always this kind of leap into 'that will make our democracy and news systems stronger.' And I don't know if that's necessarily the case," Mihailidis says.

Some research does hint that news literacy approaches could have these broader beneficial effects. In a 2017 study of 397 adults, researchers found that people who were more media-literate were less likely to endorse conspiracy theories compared with people who were less media-literate. "We can't definitely say news literacy causes you to reject conspiracy theories, but the fact that we see a positive relationship there tells us there's something to this that we need to continue to explore," says co-author Seth Ashley, an associate professor of journalism and media studies at Boise State University.

While Ashley's results are encouraging, some experts worry that a focus only on evaluating Web sites and news articles is too narrow. "News literacy in a lot of ways focuses on credibility and whether we know something is true or not, and that's a really important question, but that is one question," says Michelle Ciulla Lipkin, executive director of the National Association for Media Literacy Education. "Once we figure out if it's false or true, what is the other assessment and the other analyzing we need to do?" Determining credibility of the information is just the first step, she argues. Students should also be thinking about why the news is being told in a particular way, whose stories are being told and whose are not, and how the information is getting to the news consumer.

Pressing students to be skeptical about all information also may have unexpected downsides. "We think that some approaches to media literacy not only don't work but might actually backfire by increasing students' cynicism or exacerbating misunderstandings about the way news media work," says Peter Adams, senior vice president of education at the News Literacy Project. Students may begin to "read all kinds of nefarious motives into everything." Adams's concern was amplified by danah boyd, a technology scholar at Microsoft Research and founder and president of the Data & Society research institute, in a 2018 talk at the South by Southwest media conference. Boyd argued that although it is good to ask students to challenge their assumptions, "the hole that opens up, that invites people to look for new explanations, that hole can be filled in deeply problematic ways." Jordan Russell, a high school social studies teacher in Bryan, Tex., agrees. "It's very easy for students to go from healthy critical thinking to unhealthy skepticism" and the idea that everyone is lying all the time, he says.

To avoid these potential problems, Ashley advocates for broad approaches that help students develop mindsets in which they become comfortable with uncertainty. According to educational psychologist William Perry of Harvard University, students go through various stages of learning. First children are black-and-white thinkers–they think there are right answers and wrong answers. Then they develop into relativists, realizing that knowledge can be contextual. This stage can be dangerous, however. It is the one where, as Russell notes, people can come to believe there is no truth. Ashley adds that when students think everything is a lie, they also think there is no point in engaging with difficult topics.

With news literacy education, the goal is to get students to the next level, "to that place where you can start to see and appreciate the fact that the world is messy, and that's okay," Ashley says. "You have these fundamental approaches to gathering knowledge that you can accept, but you still value uncertainty, and you value ongoing debates about how the world works." Instead of driving students to apathy, the goal is to steer them toward awareness and engagement.

Schools still have a long way to go before they get there, though. One big challenge is how to expand these programs so they reach everyone, especially kids in lower-income school districts, who are much less likely to receive any news literacy instruction at all. And teachers already have so much material they have to impart–can they squeeze in more, especially if what they have to add is nuanced and complex? "[We] desperately need professional development and training and support for educators because they're not experts in the field," Adams says. "And it's the most complex and fraught and largest information landscape in human history."

In 2019 Senator Amy Klobuchar of Minnesota introduced the Digital Citizenship and Media Literacy Act into the U.S. Senate, which, if passed, would authorize $20 million to create a grant program at the Department of Education to help states develop and fund media literacy education initiatives in K–12 schools. More investment in this kind of education is critical if America's young people are going to learn how to navigate this new and constantly evolving media landscape with their wits about them. And more research is necessary to understand how to get them there. At the Center for News Literacy, Schneider plans to conduct a trial soon to determine how his course shapes the development of news literacy, civic engagement and critical thinking skills among students in middle school and high school.

But many more studies will be needed for researchers to reach a comprehensive understanding of what works and what doesn't over the long term. Education scholars need to take "an ambitious, big step forward," Schneider says. "What we're facing are transformational changes in the way we receive, process and share information. We're in the middle of the most profound revolution in 500 years."

About the Author

Melinda Wenner Moyer, a contributing editor at Scientific American, *is the author of* How to Raise Kids Who Aren't Assholes: Science-Based Strategies for Better Parenting—From Tots to Teens *(G. P. Putnam & Sons, 2021).*

Private Smarts: Can Digital Assistants Work Without Prying into Our Lives?

By Bryan Gardiner

Whether it is used to out-bluff world poker champions or schedule hairdresser appointments in a (mostly) convincing human voice, AI and its underlying machine-learning algorithms keep making big strides in their capabilities–and into ever-more intimate spaces of our lives. And, like any technological feat predicated on the collection and analysis of massive data sets, some of these breakthroughs come with significant privacy risks. New data-collecting techniques, however, could enable researchers to better preserve users' privacy yet still glean valuable insights from their personal information.

Take digital assistants, where the fruits of AI innovation are increasingly manifested. Today, Amazon's Alexa and Google Assistant distinguish between the voices of different people in your home, and can use these voice signatures to deliver personalized traffic reports and schedule appointments in the relevant speaker's calendar. Pulling off such tricks requires sophisticated natural-language processing skills. It also requires access to very sensitive data. Location history, contacts, calendars, transcribed records of voice queries, online browsing and purchase histories–all this can go into training the AI that helps virtual assistants become more useful and personalized.

This presents a thorny question for the companies making them, particularly if they claim to take user privacy seriously. How does one create smart virtual assistants that understand individual user preferences, without snooping on users' activities and putting their personal data at risk? "The first line of defense is anonymization and encryption of the data," says Oren Etzioni, chief executive officer of the Allen Institute for Artificial Intelligence. "Anonymization so that it's not directly linked to you in an obvious way, and encryption so that an outside party can't get access to that [information]."

In addition to offering full-disk encryption that encodes all of the information on a particular device to protect it from prying eyes, Apple and Google also rely on a statistical method known as local differential privacy to keep the data they mine from those devices anonymous. "The idea is that when it's being collected from users on their laptops or smartphones, some amount of carefully calibrated noise is also added to the data," says Anupam Datta, a Carnegie Mellon University professor of electrical and computer engineering. "That masked, noisy data from lots of users then gets encrypted and sent to Google or Apple servers to be parsed for meaningful results." The companies might learn, for example, that a certain number of smartphones use a particular app at a given time of day–but the companies would not know the identities of those smartphones or their owners.

Apple says it uses this privacy safeguard for projects such as improving the intelligence and usability of features including QuickType word and emoji suggestions in its operating system. Similarly, Google has used local differential privacy to remotely collect data from its Chrome browser operating on user devices. That process helps the company ferret out malware threats to its browser. Still, Datta warns it is a mistake to think of differential privacy as synonymous with total privacy. "It's a relative guarantee, not an absolute one," he says.

In an effort to keep sensitive user data off of remote servers entirely, Google is experimenting with an approach called federated learning. Instead of collecting and sending data to train its machine-learning models, the company sends the models themselves directly to the user. You download the current training model to your smartphone, the model changes based on what it learns from your personal data and then this updated model goes back to the cloud and is averaged in with all the other updated models. At no point does Google see or collect your personal data.

Despite such measures, some security researchers still have reservations. They point out, for example, hackers can easily reverse engineer user data if they get access to the machine-learning models. Furthermore, strategies like differential privacy are really only useful for learning generalized trends about a large group or population, says University of Southern California professor and former Google research scientist Aleksandra Korolova. These strategies, she says, do not reveal key insights at the level of the individual–which is presumably what digital assistants would most need to do.

The biggest problem is that all these techniques effectively amount to building software walls around data, according to University of California, Berkeley, professor and security researcher Raluca Ada Popa. "Attackers always end up breaking into software, so these walls will never be a foolproof mechanism," she says.

Popa and some of her colleagues at Berkeley's RISELab think they have a better solution for gleaning insights from highly personal data. Secure multiparty computation purportedly would enable tech companies to gather the information they want from multiple encrypted data sources without those sources having to reveal their private data. In effect, researchers can study information contained in large encrypted data sets without needing to see the raw data in those sets. Whether it is finding better cancer treatment predictors or serving personalized ads and restaurant recommendations, companies would not even have to see–and could not, even if they wanted to–the underlying personal information. "I really think this is the future, because you don't have to give up your data anymore to do all this useful AI and machine learning," Popa says.

Amazon, Apple, Google, Microsoft and other big tech companies may have different business models and data-collection motivations, yet all have staked their futures on increasing the intelligence of their devices and services. That means their data-collection efforts will likely only increase–and as many people have discovered in recent months, the amount of personal information these companies already have is often staggering. Someday it may be possible to train highly accurate, highly personalized AI using private data without compromising user privacy. But for now, there is only one way to ensure your sensitive information does not end up in the wrong hands: Don't share it.

Researchers Model Online Hate Networks in Effort to Battle Them

By David Noonan

The Christchurch mosque shootings, which left 51 dead and 49 injured on March 15, were a modern-day horror by any measure–from the pain and suffering of the 100 victims to the agony of their hundreds of family members and friends and the howls of grief and outrage from a wounded city and country. Now, as if all that were not nightmare enough, George Washington University researcher Neil Johnson and his colleagues point out in a new paper that, in the sum of its details, the Christchurch massacre epitomizes the border-defying complexity of what they call "online hate ecology," the global networks that link groups of neo-Nazis, white supremacists and other extremists.

In this case, Johnson and his colleagues explain in the paper, the man charged in the attack is Australian, the shootings took place in New Zealand, and the guns were covered in "messages in several European languages on historical topics that are mentioned in online hate clusters across continents." Those topics included historical defeats of Islamic forces at the hands of Europeans.

In addition, the attack on the first of the two targeted mosques was livestreamed by the shooter on Facebook. And less than five months later, on August 3, shortly before 22 people were killed and more than two dozen injured in a shooting at an El Paso, Tex., Walmart, the man charged with capital murder in that case is believed to have posted a statement online that began by saying, "In general, I support the Christchurch shooter and his manifesto."

As that litany of links suggests, Johnson says, the "networks of networks" that spread hate around the world with the click of a mouse and that can nurture mass murderers such as the Christchurch and El Paso gunmen, transcend physical and mental barriers. "They jump continents, they jump cultures, they jump languages," he says.

"We see 'Franco nationalists' in Spain connecting with 'lovers of Aryan women' in Nordic countries, then immediately flipping back to Virginia, where they're talking about militia groups."

In the new paper, published this week in *Nature*, Johnson, a professor of physics who studies complexity in real-world systems, and his team explain why disrupting and degrading such networks is so difficult. They describe the "collective online adaptations" the groups use to thwart efforts to identify and banish them.

Using public data, the researchers write, they were able to observe the networks "rapidly rewiring and self-repairing at the micro level when attacked." In the wake of the high school shooting in Parkland, Fla., in February 2018, for example, "the ecology of the [Ku Klux Klan] on VKontakte," a Russian social media platform, underwent significant, spontaneous reorganization (with old bonds among groups broken and new bonds formed) in an apparent protective response to news reports of the accused shooter's interest in the KKK.

"It's an intriguing, contrarian paper," says Susan Benesch, a faculty associate at the Berkman Klein Center for Internet & Society at Harvard University and founder and director of the Dangerous Speech Project. "The authors have tried to discover the consequences of deleting posts or accounts, which is itself a contribution, since it is too often assumed that deletion is the most effective response to bad content–without evidence."

In addition to describing the Darwinian resilience of online hate groups when targeted by Facebook and other social media platforms, the researchers suggest specific interventions, based on their mathematical modeling, that, they write, "can help to defeat online hate." And they argue that policing hate within a single platform, such as Facebook, may actually "make matters worse."

To illustrate the latter point, Johnson uses a lawn-care analogy: "If there's an infestation problem on your block, and you just focus on your own yard, you may do a really good job of eradicating stuff from your yard," he says. "But in some sense, you've reinforced what's just outside your yard, because you've pushed it back. And you've forced it to concentrate on the border of your yard, the border of your control."

The paper describes how, after Facebook banned KKK groups and the Ukrainian government subsequently banned VKontakte, clusters of Ukrainian KKK groups migrated to Facebook with "Ku Klux Klan" written in Cyrillic, making them harder to detect with English-language algorithms. Johnson calls this type of adaptation "hate-cluster reincarnation." The research also suggests the lack of coordinated policing by various platforms can lead to the creation of isolated, online "dark pools," where hate can flourish on the less policed platforms.

To counter hate groups' ability to adapt to attacks, the paper proposes first that, because large groups and clusters form from smaller ones, social media platforms should target the smaller groups (which are more numerous and easier to find) to prevent the formation of the larger ones. A second, similar suggestion in the study recommends randomly banning "a small fraction of individual users across the online hate population" rather than banning well-known hate-group leaders. As Johnson explains, this approach not only avoids the creation of martyrs, it can seriously weaken a group. "Our models show that randomly banning 10 percent of individuals can lead to a reduction in size of the global hate network by as much as 50 percent," he says.

The researchers' third policy proposal involves the creation of artificial antihate accounts by platform managers to help such groups find one another and to encourage the formation of antihate clusters to neutralize ones devoted to hate. And their fourth proposal seeks to exploit hate-group infighting by introducing a third population of users to foment dissension within a given group.

For her part, Benesch questions the suggestion that Internet platforms create artificial antihate accounts–bots, she presumes–to give rise to clusters of real accounts that would neutralize hateful clusters. "I wonder how the neutralizing would work," she says, "since my own research suggests that exposing hateful accounts to antihate material doesn't automatically neutralize them and can only deepen their commitment to hatred."

Johnson views his and his colleagues' suggested tactics as "organic" alternatives to more oppressive, Orwellian options. "The easiest way to remove hate is to just shut down all the networks," he says. "But such top-down approaches come with a cost in terms of perception. So we want to explore bottom-up approaches."

Johnson acknowledges that such methods might seem beyond what tech companies would be willing to do. But if the approaches are shown to be effective, he says, they could potentially save the companies some of the millions they spend on policing costs, not to mention the huge fines they are subject to if they are found to be in violation of the hate speech laws that more countries are adopting. "It's like having to buy more and more things to take care of the weeds," Johnson says, reverting to his lawn-care analogy. "So if I can do it organically, it may be cheaper."

About the Author

David Noonan is a freelance writer specializing in science and medicine.

Why Social Media Makes Us More Polarized and How to Fix It

By Damon Centola

Every time I log onto Facebook, I brace myself. My newsfeed–like everyone else's I know–is filled with friends, relatives and acquaintances arguing about COVID-19, masks and Trump. Facebook has become a battleground among partisan "echo chambers." But what is it about social media that makes people so polarized?

To find out, my colleagues and I ran a social media experiment in which we divided Democrats and Republicans into "echo chambers," or small groups whose members affiliate with just one political party. Next, we picked the most polarizing issues we could think of: immigration, gun control and unemployment. We asked each participant what they thought of those issues, then let people talk to each other and revise their opinions. After several rounds of discussion and revision, we evaluated each group's viewpoint.

To our surprise, the echo chambers did not make people more polarized, but less. After interacting in social networks with likeminded peers, each echo chamber–Republican and Democrat–had adopted a more moderate opinion. All groups independently moved toward opinions that were closer to the opinions on the "opposite" side of the political spectrum.

As a scientist who studies networks, I'm used to being surprised by the results of my experiments. Technology has allowed us to access more information and data about people's social networks, debunking many of our assumptions about human behavior. But even my team at the Network Dynamics Group was surprised: Why did our social media experiment find the opposite of what happens all the time in the real world of social media?

The answer lies in something social media has amplified: "influencers."

By now, most of us have a fairly specific understanding of what an "influencer" is. The word conjures up a young, wealthy person whose lifestyle is sponsored by brands like Instagram, TikTok or YouTube. But the word has a very specific network science meaning. In social media, networks tend to be centralized: a small number of people, or perhaps just one person, at the "center" of the network is connected to lots of other people in the "periphery." The multitudes in the periphery of the social network have only a modest number of connections, while the few–the so-called "influencers"–at the center of the network are connected to nearly everyone. This puts these people into the powerful position of being able to exert a disproportionate level of "influence" over the group.

By contrast, the networks used in our study were "egalitarian"–the opposite of centralized. In an egalitarian network, everyone has an equal number of contacts, and therefore influence, throughout the network.

The key feature of an egalitarian network is that new ideas and opinions can emerge from anywhere in the community and spread to everyone. But in centralized networks–like many social media sites–ideas are filtered through, or sometimes even blocked, by a powerful social influencer. As I show in my upcoming book *Change: The Power in the Periphery to Make Big Things Happen*, centralized and egalitarian networks have very different effects on partisan bias and the acceptance of new ideas.

In a centralized echo chamber, if the influencer at the middle shows even a small amount of partisan bias, it can become amplified throughout the entire group. But in egalitarian networks, ideas spread based on their quality, and not the person touting them. There is a lot of wisdom in network peripheries, in regular people with good ideas. When the social network enables those people to talk with each other, new thinking that challenge a group's biases can take hold and spread.

To see how egalitarian networks might affect other kinds of contentious issues, we conducted another experiment with smokers and nonsmokers discussing the risks of cigarette smoking. The effects were the same as with the partisan study. Both groups moved toward a more accurate understanding of smoking risks. Moreover, when participants were interviewed after the study, they reported having developed higher opinions of the other. Both smokers and nonsmokers had come to view the other group as more reasonable and trustworthy about the risks of smoking. But the exchange of ideas and eradication of bias only works when networks are egalitarian.

The problem of partisan bias is exacerbated on social media because online networks are often organized around a few key influencers. This feature of social media is one of the main reasons why misinformation and fake news has become so pervasive. In centralized networks, biased influencers have a disproportionate impact on their community—enabling small rumors and suppositions to become amplified into widespread misconceptions and false beliefs.

Our country has been struggling with bias and polarization a long time. But the issue is about to get much more urgent. As the debate over COVID-19 vaccination heats up, biased viewpoints will undoubtedly become entrenched in communities with powerful influencers at their center. If we want to eradicate, or at least lessen the impacts of the coronavirus, we should rethink how our online communities operate. The solution to the problem of vaccine hesitancy is not to eliminate echo chambers. Rather, it is to be intentional about the social networks in those echo chambers. The more equity in people's social networks, the less biased and more informed groups will become—even when those groups start off with highly partisan opinions.

About the Author

Damon Centola, Ph.D., is a professor at the Annenberg School for Communication and the School of Engineering and Applied Sciences at the University of Pennsylvania, where he is director of the Network Dynamics Group. His new book is Change: The Power in the Periphery to Make Big Things Happen *(Blackstone, 2021).*

Why Moral Emotions Go Viral Online

By Ana P. Gantman, William J. Brady and Jay Van Bavel

Social media is changing the character of our political conversations. As many have pointed out, our attention is a scarce resource that politicians and journalists are constantly fighting to attract, and the online world has become a primary trigger of our moral outrage. These two ideas, it turns out, are fundamentally related. According to our forthcoming paper, words that appeal to one's sense of right and wrong are particularly effective at capturing attention, which may help explain this new political reality.

It occurred to us that the way people scroll through their social media feeds is very similar to a classic method psychologists use to measure people's ability to pay attention. When we mindlessly browse social media, we are rapidly presenting a stream of verbal stimuli to ourselves. Psychologists have been studying this issue in the lab for decades, displaying to subjects a rapid succession of words, one after another, in the blink of an eye. In the lab, people are asked to find a target word among a collection of other words. Once they find it, there's a short window of time in which that word captures their attention. If there's a second target word in that window, most people don't even see it–almost as if they had blinked with their eyes open.

There is an exception: if the second target word is emotionally significant to the viewer, that person will see it. Some words are so important to us that they are able to capture our attention even when we are already paying attention to something else.

We thought that perhaps moral words might be special in just this way, grabbing our attention even when it was allocated elsewhere. Indeed, we have previously found that people seem highly attuned to moral stimuli in the world around them. This result could help explain why people share certain moral content online: the words that appeal to our morality break through the noise on social media.

To test this idea, we ran a pair of experiments in the lab, using a task that intentionally mimicked Twitter feeds. People were presented with a rapid stream of fictitious tweets with different types of words used for a hashtag. We found that moral words (such as crime, mercy, right), emotional words (such as afraid, love, weep) and moral-emotional words (such as abuse, honor, spite) captured more attention than neutral ones (such as coast, novel, maze). This was even true when people had been focused on a prior term. That is, these moral and emotional words broke through the noise and grabbed subjects' attention.

We then examined how this finding relates to sharing on Twitter. We analyzed a large data set containing Twitter conversations about political topics (specifically, gun control, same-sex marriage and climate change). These conversations were part of a previous paper we published, showing that messages with moral-emotional words were 20 percent more likely to be shared by another person on Twitter. We then asked whether the words that captured attention in the lab were the same ones that went viral on Twitter.

We analyzed nearly 50,000 Tweets that used words we had studied in our experiments. Some of them strongly captured attention, as measured by our attention task in the lab. Others were hardly noticeable. Most importantly, attentional capture was a robust predictor of sharing messages with these same words online. Moral and emotional words (such as lewd, kill, evil, faith and sin) were the most captivating. When they were embedded in tweets, they were significantly more likely to be shared as compared with neutral words. This was particularly striking because our measure of attention was based on an entirely different group of people than those who retweeted the messages.

Perhaps as a result of so much moral content vying for our attention on Twitter, many of us associate the platform with negative moral experiences such as outrage. But positive moral messages also gain traction on social media. For instance, after same-sex marriage rights were upheld by the U.S. Supreme Court, the hashtag

#lovewins became an instant conversation device in which people from around the globe shared an outpouring of joy.

With political conversations increasingly taking place in our social media feeds, it is especially valuable to understand what captivates us. Although it is difficult to control what gains our attention, once we know that appeals to morality pop out to us, we can be more mindful about how we interact with our Twitter feeds. We can choose what we spend extra time reading and what we decide to share.

About the Authors

Ana Gantman is an assistant professor of psychology at Brooklyn College. She studies the process of moralization–how our preferences come to be our values–and its consequences for behavior, cognition and perception. You can learn more about her research at www.anagantman.com.

William J. Brady is a National Science Foundation postdoctoral fellow in the Department of Psychology at Yale University. He studies the psychological processes that drive people's interactions during moral and political engagement online and how digital environments shape the expression of emotion and our moral values.

Jay Van Bavel is an assistant professor of psychology and director of the Social Identity and Morality Laboratory at New York University. He studies how our collective concerns–group identities, moral values and political beliefs–alter our perceptions and evaluations of the world around us.

GLOSSARY

causality The influence one event or object has over a particular effect, in which one causes the other.

compulsive Related to an irresistible urge.

correlate To have a connection between two things in which one affects or is dependent upon the other.

deleterious Harmful or damaging.

detrimental Causing harm.

dopamine A neurotransmitter produced by the brain that plays an important role in pleasure and motivation.

egalitarian Promoting the principle that all people are equal and deserve the same opportunities.

electroencephalography Measurement and recording of electrical activity in different parts of the brain.

empathy One's ability to understand and feel what another person is feeling.

empirical Based on verifiable observations; factual.

eudaemonic Causing or encouraging long-term happiness.

hedonic Causing momentary pleasure or pleasant sensations.

longitudinal A scientific study that examines the same individual multiple times over a period of time to observe any changes that may occur over that time.

pervasive Widespread among a group of people, especially something negative.

plasticity The brain's ability to change its neural networks through reorganizing and growing in response to stimuli.

prefrontal cortex The part of the brain that is located at the front of the frontal lobe and plays an essential role in making decisions, inhibiting impulses, solving problems, enabling comprehension, and reasoning.

quantitative Measured by something's quantity, or numerical value, instead of its quality.

ramification A consequence caused by an event or activity, especially a negative one.

restorative Capable of restoring health or well-being.

vocational Related to a job, employment, or an occupation.

FURTHER INFORMATION

Hughes, Virginia. "Does Social Media Make Teens Unhappy? It May Depend on Their Age," *New York Times*, March 28, 2022, https://www.nytimes.com/2022/03/28/science/social-media-teens-mental-health.html.

Kamenetz, Anya. "The Scientific Debate Over Teens, Screens, and Mental Illness," NPR, August 27, 2019, https://www.npr.org/2019/08/27/754362629/the-scientific-debate-over-teens-screens-and-mental-health.

McCauley, Robert N. "Smartphones, Social Media, and Adolescent Loneliness," *Psychology Today*, August 3, 2021, https://www.psychologytoday.com/us/blog/why-religion-is-natural-and-science-is-not/202108/smartphones-social-media-and-adolescent.

Newport, Cal. "The Question We've Stopped Asking About Teen-Agers and Social Media," *New Yorker*, November 9, 2021, https://www.newyorker.com/culture/office-space/the-question-weve-stopped-asking-about-teen-agers-and-social-media.

Popper, Nathaniel. "Panicking About Your Kids' Phones? New Research Says Don't," *New York Times*, January 17, 2020, https://www.nytimes.com/2020/01/17/technology/kids-smartphones-depression.html.

Resnick, Brian. "Have Smartphones Really Destroyed a Generation? We Don't Know," Vox, May 16, 2019, https://www.vox.com/science-and-health/2019/2/20/18210498/smartphones-tech-social-media-teens-depression-anxiety-research.

Sample, Ian. "Social Media May Affect Girls' Mental Health Earlier than Boys', Study Finds," *Guardian*, March 28, 2022, https://www.theguardian.com/science/2022/mar/28/social-media-may-affect-girls-mental-health-earlier-than-boys-study-finds.

Twenge, Jean M. "Have Smartphones Destroyed a Generation?" *Atlantic*, September 2017, https://www.theatlantic.com/magazine/archive/2017/09/has-the-smartphone-destroyed-a-generation/534198/.

CITATIONS

1.1 Are Smartphones Really Destroying the Lives of Teenagers? by Carlin Flora (February 1, 2018); 1.2 Social Media Has Not Destroyed a Generation by Lydia Denworth (November 1, 2019); 1.3 6 Reasons Smartphones Won't Replace Our Brains by David Pogue (August 1, 2013); 1.4 Generation Z: Online and at Risk? by Nicholas Kardaras (September 1, 2016); 1.5 Media Multitasking Disrupts Memory, Even in Young Adults by Bret Stetka (October 28, 2020); 1.6 How GPS Weakens Memory—and What We Can Do About It by Mar Gonzalez-Franco, Gregory Dane Clemenson and Amos Miller (May 7, 2021); 1.7 Your Brain on Google Maps by Zeynep Tufekci (October 1, 2019); 1.8 Tech Dealers Now Trying to Save the Tech "Addicts" They've Created by Larry Greenemeier (February 19, 2018); 1.9 The Reading Brain in the Digital Age: Why Paper Still Beats Screens by Ferris Jabr (November 1, 2013); 2.1 Want to Ease the Isolation of Social Distancing? Ask a Teenager by Alexandra O. Cohen (April 5, 2020); 2.2 The Death of Social Reciprocity in the Era of Digital Distraction by Brian Solis (August 8, 2019); 2.3 The Technology of Kindness by Jamil Zaki (August 6, 2019); 2.4 For a Better Connection, Talk Instead of Typing by Amit Kumar (December 15, 2020); 2.5 The Benefits of Being Yourself Online by Erica R. Bailey and Sandra Matz (February 9, 2021); 2.6 Stretched Too Thin by Social Media by Brett Frischmann (January 10, 2020); 2.7 How to Silence Cyberbullying by Elizabeth Svoboda (November 1, 2014); 3.1 Social Notworking: Is Generation Smartphone Really More Prone to Unhappiness? by Angus Chen (December 13, 2017); 3.2 School-Based Online Programs Instruct Pupils About Good Mental Health by Shekhar Saxena and Anisha Padukone (September 14, 2021); 3.3 Texting Thumb, Trigger Finger, Gamer's Thumb and Other Smartphone Injuries by Carolyn Barber (November 19, 2021); 3.4 The Double-Edged Sword of Technology for LGBTQ+ Teens by Danielle Ramo (June 23, 2020); 3.5 Mining Social Media Reveals Mental Health Trends and Helps Prevent Self-Harm by Rotem Kopel (September 14, 2021); 3.6 Green with Facebook Envy, Red with Twitter Rage by Tori Rodriguez and Maggie Puniewska (March 1, 2016); 3.7 Kids Are Not Hurt by Screen Time by Jared Rizzi (September 16, 2019); 3.8 How Consumers and Health Care Providers Can Judge the Quality of Digital Mental Health Tools by Ian Hickie and Cameron Fox (September 14, 2021); 4.1 Welcome to the Ultimate Neuroscience Lab: Your Smartphone by Karen Rommelfanger and Álvaro Fernández Ibáñez (September 14, 2021); 4.2 Schoolkids Are Falling Victim to Disinformation and Conspiracy Fantasies by Melinda Wenner Moyer (February 1, 2022); 4.3 Private Smarts: Can Digital Assistants Work Without Prying into Our Lives? by Bryan Gardiner (June 6, 2018); 4.4 Researchers Model Online Hate Networks in Effort to Battle Them by David Noonan (August 21, 2019); 4.5 Why Social Media Makes Us More Polarized and How to Fix It by Damon Centola (October 15, 2020); 4.6 Why Moral Emotions Go Viral Online by Ana P. Gantman, William J. Brady and Jay Van Bavel (August 20, 2019).

Each author biography was accurate at the time the article was originally published.

INDEX